To Sandra

Hope you enjoy!
Love
Sharon
x

Coffee Break
Companion

S. L. Grigg

ISBN-13: 978-1545430248 (CreateSpace-Assigned)
ISBN-10: 1545430241

DEDICATION

For Bazz, Lee, Alex and Belle.

CONTENTS

CONTENTS CONTINUED

1. ICE CAVERN

Finally, we had found it, the Ice Cavern. We lift our paddles out of the water and rest them on our knees as we let the boat drift and admire the beauty surrounding us.

Over an hour has passed since we entered the dark cavern mouth, now light surrounds us as though we were not deep beneath a glacier, but on top of the world. How so much light is capable of seeping through is a wonder. I gaze in amazement, it is better than I ever imagined.

Each stalactite and stalagmite is glistening a brilliant blue, the shade of the clearest, brightest, sapphire. Even the freezing water beneath us has the same gemstone brilliance. You could almost pluck an icicle and hang it on a chain – it would be the most stunning piece of jewellery.

'Let's get some pictures,' Tom say's to me as he reaches into the container by his feet to find the camera.

As he fiddles with the camera settings so we can get the best shots possible, I notice something in the ice not far ahead of us, a large, dark shape I want to study further.

'Can you see that Tom?' I ask, pointing to the patch of ice.

'What is it? I can't make it out. Shall we get closer?'

'Yeah, there's definitely something in the ice there,' I say picking up my paddle.

Tom secures the camera around his neck and lifts his paddle. Together we make a few smooth strokes into the water to bring us closer to the mysterious object.

At first, it'd still difficult to make out what is hidden beneath the ice, frozen and trapped. As we pull along the water, a shiver creeps down my spine, I have never seen anything like this before.

A creature is within the ice, only it isn't frozen or trapped as we suspected, it's moving, very slowly but moving. It is black, and hairless, from what I can see, about the height of a door and slender almost snake like, but it has limbs, so maybe more like a lizard than a snake.

'Holy crap! What the hell is that thing?' Tom exclaims, and the creature appears to stop its movement at the sound of his voice echoing through the cavern. What I presume is its head lifts, and turns in our direction.

'Shh, Tom, I think it heard you!' I gasp in a harsh whisper, as the thing presses its hideous face against the ice wall separating it from us.

Double rows of razor-like teeth show as it curls its lips up in what looks like a smile. I smell its breath as it passes straight through the ice as though there's none there. The scent of rot and decay fills the air.

'I think we should get out of here,' I whisper to Tom who is busying himself with the camera.

'Just a few shots first,' he whispers back. 'It's behind the ice, we'll be okay. We can't go without any pictures after coming all this way.'

'I don't know, can you smell that? I don't think that ice will keep it from us, and it doesn't look very friendly'

'I think you're worrying too much, sure I can smell something, it's probably just something that died down here, and that thing looks pretty freaky, but honestly what's it going to do?' Tom has stopped whispering and his voice has clearly attracted the things attention again. It presses against the ice now, as if smelling us and deciding what to do.

Tom starts taking pictures, the cavern truly is beautiful – everything looks as if it is pure crystal, so clean and clear. Everything except the creature, that is. I cannot stop watching the thing. Black, hairless and utterly grotesque.

After a few minutes of hovering close to the wall near us it backs away and I breathe a sigh of relief that it's leaving us.

Tom turns back to face the wall, having finished taking shots in each other direction.

'Why didn't you tell me it was going? I wanted to get some pictures of it. We might have discovered a new species here …'

'Sorry, I wasn't thinking, I was just too relieved to see it go.'

'Damn, Lisa. Now what do we do?'

'Just go, please, that thing creeped me out.'

'I dunno, this cavern still goes deeper, who knows what else we could find.'

'That's exactly what I'm worried about.'

As Tom laughs, a peculiar sound echoes around us and a crack begins to form in the ice wall right where the creature had been.

'Look at that, be quiet and let's go now!' I curse beneath my breath and start to paddle quickly in the direction from which we came. Tom stumbles, almost dropping the camera as my rowing makes him fall back to his seat.

'Jeez, Lisa … …' he begins just as a huge shadow crashes through the ice, sending glass-like shards raining over us. It vanishes beneath the water sending large ripples that rock our boat, knocking my oar out of my hands into the now murky depths. Fear consumes me, and I sink to the floor in the middle of the boat, pulling Tom to me.

The silence and beauty of the cavern are lost, overpowered by the stench and noise of the stalactites crashing down around us. Seeing this happening, I look up and just in time, I push Tom away as a massive blade of ice drops right where we sit. It pierces through the boat, and freezing water starts to flow through the hole it makes.

'We're going to die here, Tom!' I cry out, just before we are both thrown into the numbing liquid by something bashing into the underside of our vessel.

I struggle to surface, and Tom is nowhere to be seen. I call out for him into the emptiness, but no reply comes back, and I realise it never will, a redness that can only be blood is staining the water around me.

I feel something brush against my leg and close my eyes tight as I am yanked downwards by an unseen force. Water floods into my screaming mouth and pain shoots through me as the creature begins to rip my body apart.

2. POEM – BELONGING

When you feel you don't belong

There's nowhere you fit in

Always you just tag along

Never invited to join in

Always on the outside

You watch them grow

You just want to curl and hide

So they will never know

Groups and gatherings

Fun nights out and in

Even if you are there

You're just a shadow to them

Will you ever find a place?

Will someone let you in?

Or will you always be the face

On the outside looking in?

Always feeling so alone

In a room full of laughter

Do they see you're on your own?

Does it even matter?

You don't belong

You never did

3. LITTLE MISS PERFECT

Twirl, twirl, clap, kick, and catch the baton under my leg.

And march. Right, right, left, right left. The rhythm repeats in my head.

I catch my breath as I listen for it and, yes there it is; a roaring cheer from the crowd, the first of the night, they love me, if only I could make Cody roar for me that way.

A leap, a spin. Give them a flash with a cartwheel.

And march again, baton twirling.

Out of the corner of my eye I can see the team warming up for the second half as I continue my solo piece, pleasing the audience. My heart flutters as I notice Cody stretching out.

My routine ends with more huge cheers from the crowd, it's the loudest they've been all night. Not surprising seeing as the game hasn't been going well. Nil to nil, neither team having a strong game. The guys need to pull something out the bag in the second half if there is to be any more cheering tonight.

I grab a bottle of water off the table, pop the cap, and take a swig as I head back to the locker room to shower. As I pass the other giggling girls, waiting to take to the pitch to open the second half, none of them gives me a pat on the back to congratulate me on an excellent performance. And it was excellent.

But being head cheerleader isn't what it's cracked up to be in the movies.

Sure, it really is a popularity contest in many ways, you must look right and be clever, little miss perfect. But that's where the popularity ends, because really, all the other girls hate that you are more beautiful than they are, and the guys are terrified of you. It's lonely at the top.

I'm Kate Lewis, the head cheerleader; long, silky, straight blonde hair, with the perfect 32-24-32 hourglass figure, long legs on a 5 feet eight, 17-year-old girl – not yet a woman. Everyone wants to be me, except they don't.

The shower sputters into life as I turn the dial, reaching in to test the temperature, when I'm sure it is just right I slip out of my uniform and step in. Eyes closed I lean my head against the back wall and let the water run down my back.

Suddenly, I am pinned against the wall, a hand over my mouth and a large, strong body pressing me to the wall. My struggles are fruitless, my feet slip on the wet floor and the arm around my middle lifts me slightly, so my toes can barely scrape the floor.

A rough, deep, voice whispers to me not to struggle, and the arm around my middle slips away.

I am frozen now, unable to move.

Time seems to stop as the unmistakable sound of a zipper sneaks in with the constant trickle of the shower, which has been turned down to a drip.

Hot, firm flesh presses against my buttocks and the fear within me grows.

This is it, I'm going to be raped.

I try to close off my mind and disappear, I'm not here, this is not me, this is not happening.

But all the wishing in the world doesn't make a mysterious saviour appear.

My breasts bash against the shower dial over and again as he viciously enters me and bangs away.

I cannot cry, I cannot scream.

I just stand there and let him have his way, as his rough hands grope around my body, his fingers probing and forcing out an orgasm I did not want to have. Orgasm's are supposed to be for pleasure.

I gasp as he finishes, releasing his load into me.

He turns me round and gives me a hard, deep kiss.

It is then that I see those puppy dog brown eyes that I had so longed for, but now they look like muddy pools, Cody is no longer the man of my dreams, but one of nightmares.

'Now, let's go win this game,' I hear him say.

He releases me and walks away. I see that several other people are in the shower room too, none of them came to my rescue, in fact, they all seemed to be laughing and cheering him on, girls and boys alike.

I curl into a ball on the shower floor, holding my knees to my aching bruised breasts and lie there for what seems like an eternity.

*

I see feet coming towards me and begin to scream, a piercing soul-wrenching scream.

Not again, please.

A hand rests gently on my shoulder and I feel a towel being placed over me, but I cannot stop screaming.

More feet, and voices I cannot make sense of from behind my screams.

I am lifted from the floor and placed on something like a bed, the screams subside into heavy sobs as blankets and straps cover me. Then the bed is moving.

Voices continue, they seem to be reassuring me in some way, but I cannot comprehend them as I slip away.

Later, I awake to the feel of starched sheets and a distinct disinfectant smell. I realise I must be in hospital. Coach is sat beside my bed, a heavy sadness pinching his face. He looks at me, as I look at him and a tear rolls down his cheek.

There are no words either of us can say that will make it better, but he points to the police officer at the end of my bed and I know at least that Cody will not get away with this. I carefully sit up and with a weak and tired voice begin to tell the story …

4. ALTER EGO

Allow me to introduce myself, I'm not sure if we have met.

I'm 'T', take that how you will. It's not my name, you know that already.

'T' for trouble.

'T' for teenager.

'T' for tears.

'T' for terrible.

Tantalize, terrorise, tart, tattoo, tear-away, tease, tantrum, temper, temptress ... ... the list goes on.

You may have caught a glimpse of me occasionally.

Other's only know this me.

Whatever your experience of 'T', you can be sure of one thing, you'll never forget me.

I come out to play when things get tough, emotions are high, and life is too much for 'her' to handle. I am the escape, the freedom, letting go, forgetting (not forgiving), fun, fun, fun ... ...

I am out of control and I love it. I can do anything, be anything, have anything, nothing is beyond my reach.

I want, want, want.

I take, take, take.

Give me your attention, don't stop. Thanks. Now I'll move on to the next one. Line up, line up I'm here for the taking, I want you to want me.

Dressed up to the nines, high as a kite. I'm going to dance all night.

Knocking back shots, smoking pot. Anything goes, for this is my show.

I flutter my lashes, wriggle my hips. Everyone watching, as they should be – don't you wish your girlfriend was a hot as me – hahaha.

I play with hearts, I play with minds, I play with bodies, including mine.

I look in the mirror and what do I see, a sexy little minx winks at me, but behind those eyes the secret lies.

The broken girl, the alter ego, the real person trapped beneath the mask. The eyes lie, the sparkle isn't there, it's lost like her.

I shake my head, straighten my hair, touch up my make-up and glare. I push her away for another day, she cannot have this she would not appreciate the effort it takes, with her emotions and feelings she is just a mess. Lock her up and throw away the key. There's too much fun to be had to waste your life being sad.

Get up and go, run and scream, dance and dream.

Tonight is my night, get me another drink. Laughing, flirting, enjoying it all.

Look at me, bad girl on the prowl, hunting a victim. Try to chase me, you may catch me, but you'll never keep me, this girl is not for taming.

Gimme your number, I'll never call. One night is all, so do not fall.

Leaving a hoard of devastation and destruction in my wake, I steal your mind, and your heart I will break. But she will be back when I awake, so no sleep tonight, try as she might. I won't let her have this back, I need to rule it, possess it. This is my night.

I am 'T', come to me, the alter ego who loves to be everything she could never be – free ... ...

Call me 'T'.

5. YOUR CALL IS IMPORTANT TO US

Jay breathed a sigh of relief as he saw the thumbs up signal, from the other side of the glass, indicating that they had finished recording. His throat was parched and the glass of warm milk which had been placed beside him was a sweet comfort. He sipped it gently and it soothed his overworked larynx.

Talking for a living is harder work than you would expect, as Jay had discovered. He had been cooped up, day after day, for three years doing this job now.

Recording messages for automated phone lines involved sitting in a cramped, soundproofed booth that felt like a large coffin after several hours.

Jay slumped onto the hard stool, wishing they had room for a comfy sofa instead. He felt as if the dark walls were closing in on him and couldn't wait to finish recording for the day, so he could escape the dreary box.

Jay's mind wandered, and he thought how someone who suffered claustrophobia might cope, feeling certain this job would be intolerable for someone like that, and relieved he didn't have that problem.

A green light flicked on beneath the glass in front of him, the cue that it was time to start the next recording. Jay took a deep breath, cleared his throat and began speaking into the microphone. Reading from the script in his hand he tried hard not to let his mind wander again.

The small room filled with his voice.

Jay was aware that he is one of those secret weapons used by companies to seduce unsuspecting callers into staying on the line longer than they would have done, a tool of distraction, used to reassure and convince callers that their call is important, and it will be worth the wait. After all, if there's one thing most people agree about, it's that automated phone lines can be the most annoying thing, when what we really want is to speak to a real person. Still, despite this, it is the sexy voice that people remember most, which is exactly what the companies want.

With his soft, Scottish lilt, Jay has the tone of a young Sean Connery, a deeply sexy accent sure to make the ladies crumble. He felt like this was even more of a deception as it conjures up an image of a suave, sophisticated, handsome gentleman which couldn't be further from Jay's own below average appearance. Short, plump, with bad skin, and a mop of ginger hair, Jay is acutely aware that his voice is his greatest asset, being the butt of many jokes from a young age. He would have loved to work in a more visual media position, such as newsreader, but he would never have made it.

Luckily this is not a job requiring great beauty, rather the voice of an Angel and as such, Jay has been a hit. His role has introduced him to the woman who is soon to become his wife and clients of the recording studio request his voice for their recordings more often than any other guy on the team. So, despite the less than favourable working conditions, the benefits it has bought forth mean that all in all it was not bad for a day's work, and it pays well too.

The light blinks red and another day's work is done.

6. POEM – TRIGGER

How many times can you twist the knife?

You always know how

To kick me when I'm already down

Trigger …

o

How much hurt can you bring to my life?

Weren't you the man

Supposed to make me your wife?

Trigger …

o

Words so cold

Cut to my soul

Eyes of ice

Watch me unfold

Trigger …

o

It takes all my strength

To stop myself falling

Into the trap

You are unfurling

To finish me

Trigger …

o

I made it through the night

Now I will make it through my life

No longer will I allow you

to

be

my

Trigger

7. 5/25 TORNADO: TOMMY'S STORY

Sheltered by a large tree, Tommy and his mum wait for the bus home after a busy morning shopping. It's cold, raining heavily, and quite a wind has built up.

'Will we be home soon, Mummy, I'm cold?'

'Not long now, Tommy. The bus will be here soon.'

'I want to play with my toys.'

'When we get home, you can play with them.'

'Will it be much longer?'

'Not much longer, Tommy, dear.'

'But I'm bored.'

*

I don't think Mummy said anything else because then the big wind happened.

It was raining loads, and we were waiting for the bus outside McDonalds then it went dark, like night time, but it was only morning. Leaves were flying round and round, like curly chips, or the way water goes down the hole in the sink.

It all happened so quick we didn't even know whether to run like everyone else or stay where we were, but we stayed.

A bus on the other side of the road, its roof was gone and there was lots of glass everywhere as it flew out of shop and car windows.

There were big bangs as the wind made it all fall out in little pieces like a jigsaw puzzle. It will take someone a long, long time to put all the glass back together again for those shops!

I open my eyes and stand up as the wind slows down; it had knocked me over and now I can't see Mommy anywhere. Mommy always tells me I should never talk to strangers, but I am so scared because I can't find her that I asked everyone who comes near me:

'Have you seen my mommy?'

I don't think Mummy will be mad at me, nobody talked to me anyway. I don't know how long it's been, it feels like all day now and I still can't find Mummy, she let go of my hand when I fell over. The big tree where we were standing is on the floor now.

When it got windy it made things bang like lots of fireworks all at once and then people were running around everywhere, screaming. Other people were lying on the floor covered with bits of roof and trees. Some of them had blood on them too, I know it was blood because it was like when I cut my knee when I fell off my bike the other day, on Sunday, now I know why Mummy said it was only a little cut on my knee, because the people lying down have a lot more blood than was on my knee.

It's scary not knowing where Mummy has gone. I have been walking around for ages trying to find her. I couldn't see her lying down or running around.

I had been lying down for a bit myself when I fell over. I hurt my head where I bumped it on the floor; my back and hair are wet and sticky like jam.

After I fell over, my ears didn't work properly, at first, it was like the bangs had switched the sound off. It made me jump when the sound came back because of everybody screaming and the shop and car alarms ringing. I have been crying a lot because I am on my own, Mommy always called me her brave little soldier and told me not to cry.

I wish mommy was here now to give me a cuddle, I'm getting cold, and sleepy, my head really hurts, the sticky dampness is getting worse, nobody will help me, and I want my mommy. I lie down again by a post-box, hopefully Mummy will come and find me soon. I'll just have a little sleep while I wait.

8. THE PURGE

I push the last bit of dinner around on my plate with the fork. I can't bear to eat another bite.

Just the smell of the tomato based sauce on the chicken is making my throat close.

I want to heave.

I glance across at my partner, whose plate is empty. I take both plates and stand up from the table.

'Chicken going straight through me again,' I say, as I scrape the remainder of my food into the bin.

My partner looks at me, eyes wide with concern, and I feel guilty for how I feel about myself when someone loves me so much, it hurts to see that look.

'You really should see the doctor about that you know, it's not good to be rushing to the toilet after every meal.'

'It's not every meal.'

'But it is getting worse, please, I'm worried about you.'

'I'll be okay, I'm gonna go for a work out after I've been to the toilet.'

'Okay, hunny, I'll wash up.'

I walk out of the kitchen, through the lounge, and head upstairs to the bathroom.

Once inside, I shut and lock the door. Catching a glimpse of myself in the full-length mirror hanging on the back of the door, I cringe at the sight. I see a scrawny legged figure, with slopping shoulders, a pot belly, and flab everywhere. My teeth are rotting, and I have constant mouth ulcers, my breath must be awful too; for those I guess my actions are to blame. It's disgusting how repulsive I am. How can my partner think this is something appealing and attractive? I turn away from the mirror unable to let that view poison my vision any longer.

Taking a length of toilet paper and lifting the seat of the toilet, I drop the paper into the bowl to muffle the sound of the splashes.

I turn around and take my toothbrush from the caddy by the sink, trying to avoid the small mirror hung directly over the sink. I turn back to the toilet, bend down, and purge.

My throat burns, and the smell stings my watering eyes as the food I have just eaten flows awkwardly back out of me. Taking another length of toilet roll, I wipe my mouth, and then take another strip to wipe my eyes before throwing both into the bowl and flushing the chain.

Turning back to the sink I wash the end of my toothbrush, return it to the holder and swill my mouth with water from the tap. A gargle of mouthwash freshens up my breath enough to hide the vomit smell, and I unlock the door.

My partner is stood outside the door, tears streaming down her face.

'I heard it all, Dominic,' she weeps, as she takes me into her arms and I cannot hold back my own tears.

9. WATERFALL

Ray leaned forward, his weight precariously balanced on the camping stool.

The glow behind the waterfall had caught his eye several minutes before, at first a reflection of the bright full moon seemed a natural explanation, but now he wasn't so sure.

The glow was growing before his eyes, taking on a form. Captivated, the marshmallows roasting over the campfire were forgotten as Ray was unable to stop staring at the vision appearing before him.

Without interrupting the flow of the water, the glowing form emerged. It was now clearly a woman. An ethereal, ghostly, beauty. Long wavy hair, such a pale blonde it appeared white with the glowing light that seemed to be emanating from within her. Her skin milk bottle white, and a flowing dress that was almost translucent clung to her melon-sized breasts. He had never seen anything so beautiful.

Despite being unable to withdraw his gaze, Ray was suddenly aware of the silence and stillness surrounding him. The feint rustle of leaves in the breeze, crackling of firewood and breathing sounds of his companions sleeping within the tent beside him, had all stopped.

The figure moved towards him, as transfixed by him as he was by her, she was gliding through the air and her mouth parted slightly as if she was about to speak.

Ray felt himself gasp as her hand lifted towards him. Mouth widening, along with piercing eyes that seemed to slice into his own.

Closer now, Ray cold feel an icy chill growing within his dense mass of a body.

Suddenly scared by the ever-stretching width of the woman's mouth, Ray opened his own mouth ready to scream.

Before he could make a sound, the maiden began to sing, a high-pitched, screech of a song, that slammed Ray's mouth shut with force.

A banshee …

Her screech filled the night air and stopped the hearts of anything that laid eyes open her, including Ray's. Her mouth now revealing sword-like rows of teeth, and stretching like a cavernous throat. Her prey gravitated towards her, pulled as though caught in a sci-fi tractor-beam, to be consumed whole.

A stick of burned marshmallows dropped at the edge of the campfire, which crackled again as the night breeze caught it. A camp stool beside it with a warm seat that betrayed it had recently been occupied, now sat empty.

In the distance a brilliant glow slowly faded behind the waterfall.

10. POEM – DON'T

Don't get close to me
It hurts

Don't love me
It hurts

Don't want me
I'll run away fast

Don't care for me
I'll run away fast

Use me
It feeds my self-hatred

Abuse me
It feeds my self-hatred

Take advantage of me
I need it

Lust after me
I need it

I'm broken
and this is how I cope

Think it's about time someone threw out a rope
To save me

Don't

11. LOST (Written aged 11)

Sally opened her eyes, where was she? What had happened?

She looked around, little Mary-Lou was sleeping peacefully next to her.

Now she remembered, the ship, the planes … …

The bombers had attacked their ship and she had grabbed Mary-Lou and jumped overboard in to one of the 'dinghies, then they had paddled away as the ship disappeared below the water. Little Mary-Lou was only six years old, she just sat there crying she didn't know what had happened.

'Sally, where's Mommy?' Sally looked around, Mary-Lou had woken up.

'It's okay, bab, ' I'm here. Look, have this.' Sally passed her some bread that she had taken from the box she wore round her neck. They were evacuees and they just had a few essentials in their little boxes and one item to carry. Food, drink, and washing items were in the box, Mary-Lou had her teddy and Sally had a first aid kit, which her mum had made her take in case either of them got hurt.

Sally sat up in the dinghy, there was land ahead. *'The sky's nice and clear, we should make it,'* she thought. There were bits of wood from the ship that had fell into the dinghy, she picked one up and started rowing towards the piece of land. Mary-Lou was playing picnics with her teddy and the piece of bread.

'Sally should be able to cope, she's 12 now,' Sally remembered her mum saying to their aunt before they went, but could she cope? She was beginning to think she wouldn't be able to.

The land was further away than Sally had first thought, as the midday sun streamed down on them like red hot pokers prodding coal.

Mary-Lou began to get very hot.

'Sally, I'm hot and I feel tired, can I have some dinner?'

'Here, bab' have this then lie down.' Sally passed her some crisps and bottled water.

'But I'm hot.'

'Take your blouse off then, you've got your vest underneath to stop you catching cold.'

Mary-Lou removed her blouse, drank some water, then ate the crisps Sally had given her.

Sally stopped rowing for a while and had a bit of bread, she didn't want to eat too much as she didn't know how long they would have to make the food last for. She didn't know how long it would take to reach civilisation.

Sally and Mary-Lou eventually fell asleep. While they slept, the dinghy drifted ashore on an island.

The sun crept across the sky, brushing the night away, and dusting the sky clean.

The water lapped against the shore bringing a small spray onto the faces of the sleeping children. Mary-Lou was the first to wake up this time, she shook Sally moaning, 'Sally, Sally wake up we aren't on the water anymore.'

Sally woke up, her eyelids fluttering open dreamily. She glanced around, and realised Mary-Lou was right. She got out of the dinghy, stretched, and hugged Mary-Lou.

'Don't worry any more, bab," she said, "we'll be all rightall right.'

They had some breakfast of dry cereal. Sally decided that they best try to find some people, but it looked like they would have to go through the forest in front of them to find a village or something. On one side of them was a huge cliff, behind them was the sea, and on the other two sides, past the beach, was forest.

They collected together their things and headed towards the forest. As they got to the top of the beach, Sally noticed there were coconuts on the closest trees. So, with a lot of effort, she shinned up one and knocked a few of the coconuts down, it was a good job she had been a tomboy back home, always climbing trees and fighting.

It had not been easy for Sally to get the coconuts from the trees, as the trees had been very high and slim, it was lucky she was as nimble as a monkey, and it was worth the effort.

She took off her cardigan and tied it around the some of the coconuts in a makeshift bag.

'These two are what we're having for today, so make it last,' she told Mary-Lou. Then she dug around to find a sharp stone and tried to crack into the top of a coconut. It took a long time to get a crack but once it was started it broke up easier then. They drank the milk from inside and then chewed on chunks which Sally broke off.

They set off into the trees.

As the sun began to slip away behind the trees they came to a small clearing.

'We'll sleep here for the night, then tomorrow we'll have to see how far we can go, okay?'

'Yes, Sally,' Mary-Lou nodded.

'Okay, now you pull up some of that moss for us to use as a bed and I'll make a fire as it's getting cold. There are some sticks over there and I have some matches in the box, so we should be all right.'

Mary-Lou gathered lots of moss and made a nice springy bed for them to sleep on. When Sally got a small fire burning, she found a small can of beans and a can opener in the box. She opened the tin and warmed it by the fire. They ate the beans and chewed some more coconut then settled on the moss to go to sleep.

Mary-Lou drifted off almost immediately, but Sally lay awake for a long time trying to figure out where they might be. Finally, she could keep her eyes open no longer, her eyelids drooped, and she fell asleep.

The night came alive with the sounds of exotic birds and insects. The trees aglow by the bright little fireflies.

Sally and Mary-Lou were lost in the middle of a forest now, but just two days walk away was a small town. As the girls slept the people of the town were holding an all-night party, celebrating the summer festival, they danced the night away.

When Mary-Lou and Sally awoke the next morning, Mary-Lou's arm was hurting. There was a huge insect bite on her arm and it was sore, Mary-Lou was crying.

'It's okay, bab, don't worry,' Sally consoled her as she sorted through the first-aid kit then dealt with the bite.

They drank some more coconut milk, then continued their journey, hoping they were heading in the right direction to find people.

After dinner, Sally tripped over some tree roots, slightly twisting and straining her ankle. She took some painkillers from the first aid kit and bandaged her ankle. She had to keep going even though her foot was killing her, they needed to find civilisation.

When they settled down that night little did they know they were now only three miles from the village. Five miles past the village was a bigger town with a hospital and airport.

'Sally, how much further have we got to go? My legs hurt, and I want Mommy.'

'Don't worry, Mary-Lou, hopefully it's not much further now,' Sally said, then thought to herself, *I wish I knew, I need to see a doctor about this ankle and we don't have much food or water left.*

They set off early the next morning hoping they would reach a town that day.

It was hard going with Sally hobbling on her bad ankle, and Mary-Lou was just sick of walking all the time.

'What's that noise?' Mary-Lou said that evening as they came close to what looked to be another clearing through the trees.

'Shh, I'll go and see.' Sally crept forward and looked through the bushes, then turned around and gave an excited squeal. She grabbed Mary-Lou and swung her round, then nearly dropped her as she cried out in pain from her foot, then she finally managed to speak , 'It's a village Mary-Lou, we're safe! At last, we might be able to get home!'

They rushed excitedly out of the bushes, pain forgotten for the moment and ran to the closest house. Sally paused as she remembered what their mum had said about not talking to strangers, but thought in this case they had to make an exception. She knocked on the door and a short woman answered.

'Yes, who are you?' she said to Sally, as she looked the dishevelled girls over, 'Where have you come from?'

'Excuse me,' Sally said 'Sorry, to disturb you but we're lost, you see the boat we were on was sunk by bombers, and then our dinghy drifted ashore, and we walked through the forest and ended up here. Can you help us please?' the words just rushed out of her mouth.

The woman looked confused, but friendly.

'Come on in and tell me about it so I can understand, it's getting late, and you wee girls look like you could use a good meal and a wash.' They followed her into the house where a group of boys and girls were sat playing on the floor. They stopped what they were doing to examine the two girls cautiously.

'It looks like you have hurt your foot too, I'll take you to the hospital in the morning and we will get you all fixed up, and find out how to get you home. But first you need some rest.'

'Thank 'you,' Sally said, 'I don't know how we will be able to repay you for helping us.'

'Don't worry, just eat up,' the woman said as she placed a large plate of food in front of the girls. They ate heartily and chatted with the woman and her children, explaining all they could that would help the woman be able to find out how to get them home. They bathed and slept comfortably at last.

The next day, the woman took them into the big town and found people that could help sort them out. They had to stay in the town until the war was over, before they could return home.

Eventually, Sally and Mary-Lou were returned home but they never forgot the wonderful family who had looked after them when they were lost. They wrote to each other for many years, until one day, when Sally was grown-up, she returned to the island to live there for good.

12 – EDITING: SWIMMING

An exercise piece, editing from approximately 150 words, down to just 50 words. See how it alters the story.

150 words

She sat on the edge of the pool, feet dangling in the water. The squeals and laughter of the children playing on the floats filled her ears. The mid-afternoon sun warming her back. Carl dove under the water to pick up the heavy block James had thrown for him. Amy paddled away from the splashes of Chloe and Anne, trying to tip her off the float.

Watching them all having fun made her smile. She stood up and walked round to the shallow end. The water here lapped against the tiles. The sloped edge of the pool almost beach-like so she could wade in slowly. Moving forward carefully, water between her toes. Each step taking her deeper until it reached her knees.

'Come on, Mom, you can do it!' Carl called out.

But, Sarah couldn't swim, the thought of going deeper made her freeze to the spot.

*

100 words

She sat, feet dangling in the water. The squeals and laughter of children playing on floats fills her ears. The afternoon sun warming her back. Carl dives under the water to pick up a heavy block.

Watching them having fun makes her smile. She walks round to the shallow end. The water lapped against the tiles. The sloped edge of the pool almost beach like. She wades in slowly, water between her toes. It reaches her knees.

'Come on, Mom, you can do it!' Carl called out.

But, Sarah 'couldn't swim, the thought of going deeper made her freeze to the spot.

*

50 words

She sat feet dangling in the water. Children squeal, playing on floats. Carl dives under making her smile. She walks to the shallow end, wades in slowly to her knees.

'Come on, Mom, you can do it!'

Sarah froze to the spot, she cannot swim.

13. EVERY LAMP IN THE CITY

Every lamp in the city was lit that night …

Except for one.

Dita found it strange that this one house was not lit like the others. The walk home, from locking up at the restaurant, to join her family in the festival celebrations was hurried, yet she maintained her observant manner.

The streets were almost empty as everyone had retired to their homes for the traditional summoning. Dita was among the stragglers, rushing to be back before the hour was upon them.

The city was small and fully occupied, for a house not to be lit was a bad omen, and this drew Dita to it. She had to know who would risk not partaking in the summoning. She felt compelled to do something about it, fearing what effect it could have if the tradition was broken. She had never known a house to fail to comply, and wondered if anyone else had noticed; but immediately realised it was unlikely – – such was the urgency for everyone to be indoors.

Dita glanced at her watch, there really 'wasn't time to investigate, and yet she could not draw herself away. A sigh as she heaved her slipping bag back on her shoulder. She started to walk up the path to the house.

With each step the darkness seemed to envelop her. A strange chill sent a shudder down her spine, and a desire to run home fleeted across her mind. Still, she continued to the veranda, all the time feeling more and more cut off from the rest of the city and drawn to continue her quest.

The top step creaked under her as she approached the front door. Glancing back, she could barely see the street below her, even though it was less than twenty feet away. Goosebumps pricked her skin as the fine hairs stood on end, was this fear?

Finally, the door was within reach, as she reached out to knock, it opened slightly, releasing a musty, damp smell. Now Dita knew she was scared, but she could not turn away. It was like a force had taken control of her actions and turning away was no longer a possibility. The only option was to go into the gloom that peered at her through the crack where the door stood ajar.

A gentle push and the door swung silently open and Dita stepped over the threshold.

Immediately a sense of ending ran through to her bones as she felt the shadows close around her. Glancing back, she saw the door close as silently as it had opened. There was no sign of life here, and as the last remaining light from the street vanished with the closing door, Dita felt a scream building in the pit of her stomach. As she opened her mouth to release the scream, the shadows poured in like air filling her mouth and lungs, trapping the scream within her. Blackness, never-ending blackness.

The summoning was done, the sacrifice was made, the lamps in the house came on.

Every lamp in the city was lit that night.

14. POEM – MY BPD EXSITENCE

I do not live
I just exist
What a view
A distorted twist
The outside world
All they can see
Pretty, happy, smiley me
Tidy house, clean and clothed
Always busy, always posed
No fresh cuts
To raise their tuts

But inside nothing matters
Torn apart she shatters
Hurt in ways even she 'can't see
Would anyone else want to be me?

Wallow
Unable to swallow
Smoke and drink to stave the hunger
Empty, numb
Disgusting, self-pity
I 'don't deserve your sympathy
Lie to myself that I am fine
Automatic pilot all the time
As long as nothing shows
Even with the hang of my clothes

Body shrinking
Mind unthinking
Write all day
But do not speak
Hideaway

Lonely
But never alone
Wearing BPD like a crown
Hate it, hate me
We're one and the same 'can't you see?
My life, my love
All one-day end
Confide your feelings in a friend
No point – – no feelings
Nothing to share
Who would understand

I take you by the hand
I look you in the eye
I 'can't even cry
My love for you, my family, my friends
This is all that is real
But still the numb pain never ends
I have no words
I have no feelings
Unreal, not here
To go to work
I now just fear

No sense
No meaning, no reason
No rhyme
Clock is ticking all the time

Smoke and smoke and smoke some more
Is anybody keeping score?
Just all of time
Drifting by
Still alive, still by your side
With love alone, my remaining strength
Unfair to all who reach out to me
Love me, want me, feel me, need me, part of me
But still I am not here
Will I ever be?
'That's what I fear

15. LONELINESS

To the outside world Karen is a happily married mother of two; cliché maybe, but that is what they see.

With long, black hair, and milky white skin, Karen has a unique style. Pretty without being too flashy, and always a smile on her face, but her smile hides what her eyes cannot. If you look carefully into the blue haze you can see sadness.

To meet Karen, you would not believe the loneliness that encompasses her, threatening to shatter her heart. Karen hides the emptiness with a proud and confident mask, a smart and successful woman. For all intents and purposes, she would have you believe that despite her burdens, she is content with her lot, and for the best part, this is true. She dearly loves her family and they love her too, but a person needs more than this to not feel alone.

This evening, however, she stands beneath the dusky glow of a waning moon, looking out across a balcony. A fountain of water spurts from a pedestal of mermaids in the hotel forecourt below. The clouds have merged as one solitary being, matching her mood, alone under a frightful sky.

Hot tears stain her cheeks with black streaks. Behind her, the bar is emptying, like her heart, as the patrons move within to watch the show on the upper floor. An hour has passed already since the time they were due to meet, a birthday outing with the girls to celebrate her thirtieth. Yet here she stands, as alone as she often feels, even in the most crowded room.

Not one of her friends has turned up, some had made their excuses beforehand, but others were crueller letting her believe they would join her.

While not within her control, the burden of her husband's life threatening, personality changing, condition has created a retreat from her by others. Almost as much as people have withdrawn from him, and his aggressive tendencies, they have left her too. Even the closest of friends and family could bear it no more, leaving Karen alone to cope with the weight of it all.

Even the moon appears to be mocking her, as the chinks fall from her superficial armour. Like the clouds above her heavy with rain, loneliness is a mood that follows Karen daily, waiting to burst.

This loneliness is Karen's curse. Even if they had bothered to turn up tonight they would not realise the role they played in making her feel so alone.

This was the reason she busied herself so entirely each day. So busy she even had to book in time on her calendar to play with her children, all this to try to escape, to cover up the loneliness by avoiding further human contact – – the fear of even more rejection too much for her to contemplate.

Karen believes that another reason for the distance some keep from her is a mixture of jealousy and fear of her personal successes, but even if this is true, it does not excuse their hurtful behaviour, she has forgiven them too many times.

'Karen's lively, friendly, appearance portrays the kind of person you would expect to be surrounded by close, caring, friends, when in fact the opposite is true.

They only get in touch when they want something, and despite their behaviour, Karen is always there for them, no matter the problem.

Eventually, the storm will break, and Karen's spirit will be broken beyond repair, but until that day she carries on and nobody notices, nobody cares.

Her husband and children are waiting for her back home, and the mask will be back in place to extol them with tales of her wonderful evening. To ensure they do not wonder why she is home so soon, she will stroll home slowly rather than get a taxi, making sure to stop along the way to repair the tear stained cheeks.

So, as the doors close and the show begins and Karen heads for home, alone.

16. THE POLE

Snaking her hips around the pole, Lily was the centre of attention. Men were drooling over her svelte figure, mouths agape as she shimmied and slithered. A perfect size six, pert little breasts, dancer's legs, and curly auburn hair, all the curves in the right places.

Being a pole dancer 'wasn't 'Lily's dream role, but it was fun, she worked hard as an accountant by day, but after the stuffiness of the office she needed a release, so her second job was more like a hobby really.

A few nights a week she pole danced until late. It bought in more money than a 'week's work in the financial world – – which is really saying something. But the money 'didn't matter to her. She loved the feel of the pole between her legs, she loved dressing up and most of all she loved watching how others watched her as she danced around the pole.

She was what you would call pure "sex on 'legs', a perfect 10 in every sense of the saying.

But Lily had a secret one could never guess by looking at her now. She was fast approaching 30 and still a virgin. You would have thought Lily could have any man she wanted being such a stunner, but Lily 'wasn't interested in men – – women were her passion. Yet even here she had an unusually low success rate when it came to seducing other women.

It was a complete mystery because 'Lily's personality was every bit as beautiful as her body. She was smart, fun, and successful in everything.

Except the one thing she desired most … … Love

17. THE INVENTOR

I watch the old man as he works, pencil moving fast across the parchment, he flicks his coarse, thick, beard over his shoulder when it gets in the way as he creates another design.

The workshop is cool as he sits in front of the wooden easel. Our linen robes protect us from the breeze coming through the open light giving holes in the stone walls.

I am charged with collecting materials from the merchants in the market. But, while he draws I watch from the haybed in the corner. With scraps of discarded parchment and a chalkstone I try to design myself, hoping one day to create something better than the objects my master creates.

Most often he will construct things from wood and animal skin, to bring his ideas to life. None of them seem to be of much use, a structure like the wings of birds and a contraption that produces hot water plumes he calls "steam".

This latest design is called a "battery" a move away from wooden structures. 'Master's creation contains metal, formed and shaped, he talks of the heat of the sun and water giving power to things.

It just seems like another thing that will end up cluttering the bottom of the workshop to me, maybe he should try to make something people might want to use?

18. POEM – CHEMISTRY

A fleeting glance across a crowded room
I notice you, noticing me
Heart flutters
Distance matters

Chemistry

Flirtation is subtle advances
Coupled with desire
For closeness
For running away

Chemistry

Longing and fear
So apart but still so near
Everyone sees
Everyone notices
Everyone comments and questions
How can we want so much?
But not touch

Chemistry

Eyes meet
Hearts beat

Chemistry

Feel the heat
Runaway fast
Pounding feet
Hide from the feelings
You cannot beat

Chemistry

19. BARFLY

He stands at the bar, a pint of Fosters in his one hand, the other gesticulating wildly as he talks to a portly, older man. The older guy is perched on a bar stool looking unimpressed with the younger guy's conversational attempts, but that doesn't stop him.

Every so often he glances across to the group sat in what is jokingly referred to as the 'Loser's Lounge', occasionally he will join them, as will most of the other regulars.

She is part of the group, currently playing a game of pool with her friend. He watches as she bends over the table to take a shot, her tight jeans stretching across her pert bottom. He tries not to stare, but he just cannot resist, and he is not the only one. He notices the other eyes drawn in her direction, from the youngest to the oldest nearly every guy in the pub enjoys watching her play.

He smirks to himself thinking how, unlike the rest of them, he has had the privilege of closer inspection of that fine piece of ass. Just as quickly though, he berates himself, never again he swore to himself. That girl was trouble with a capital T! He draws his eyes away and attempts to re-enter into banter with the older guy only to discover the seat vacated.

Turning again he sees her look in his direction, their eyes meet for a moment and he can't help but smile, knowing she knows he is watching her, and that she is watching him back. She glances down, unable to keep looking at him. He knows why, he has caused that hurt look that passed over her face when their eyes met. He can feel what she is feeling, but still he tries to hold to his resolve.

Rolling a cigarette to distract himself, all the while he can feel her eyes burning into him, but each time he glances up she quickly looks away.

This game of trying not to be caught watching each other

continues through the evening, but everyone sees it, everyone knows these two cannot resist each other. Despite all that has gone between them in the past, the trouble, the rows, the passion, the deceit, the fights. Theirs is a true love-hate relationship, that neither can break free from.

He walks out the side door of the bar to smoke his cigarette, and is greeted by the lads jeering about his most recent interaction with her, where she finally lost her temper with his cruel dismissals of her affection, and smacked him one in front of everyone.

He feels embarrassed to be laughed at and tries to shrug it off, further cruel dismissals at her expense, but the lads know better by now, and just torment him even more.

As he flicks away his cigarette end he comes to a decision. It is time to call a truce, again. They both drink here often and cannot continue to pretend they don't even know the other exists.

Returning to the bar, he sees her waiting to be served. Picking up his beer from where he left it he walks over and stands beside her. She peers at him out the corner of her eye, but acts as though she has not noticed him standing there. He props his elbows on the bar facing out towards the room as she faces the bar. He looks at her, seeing the pain in her face as she tries to pretend he isn't there. He tells her that she owes him an apology, and as she turns to face him he can see tears in her eyes.

She begins to speak to him, desperation in her voice, as she tries to explain how hurt she was by his actions, that it had pushed her to something she had never experienced before – – violence. He does not defend himself, admitting to being nasty and cruel.

He hopes that making her believe he is not worthy of her affection will keep her from getting too close to him. It is not good for either of them to be so close to the other, he knows this, but it seems she does not.

Mid-sentence, she is interrupted by the barman finally coming to serve her. Drink ordered, she turns back to him but does not continue what she was saying, she shakes her head, realising whatever she says will not be heard by him. He can see this realisation within her and they both turn away.

She takes her drink and returns to sit with her friends as he watches on from his perch at the bar.

Where do they go from here? he wonders. At least they are speaking again now, kind of. Without specifically asking for it, he has managed to bring about a truce between them for the time being. How long it will be until they are back in each other's arms, or at each other's throats, is any bodies guess. For now, though he will continue to watch her from a short distance like a fly on the wall.

He is the barfly.

20. UNDER THE SEA

Kief swam towards the rocky outcrop. The sea was calm, the waves lapping gently. Pulling himself up onto the seaweed coated mound, Kief looked at the view. Far enough from the shore that early morning dog-walkers wouldn't notice him, if they weren't specifically looking, but close enough that if she looked again, she would see and recognise him.

He waited, as he had for months now, since he first caught sight of her, and she of him. The same day every week, their eyes would meet across the short distance. She would appear from the sand dunes, removing her shoes as she stepped onto the beach. He could imagine her wriggling her toes in the cool, morning touched, sand as she hesitated every time.

After standing there for a few moments she would cross the beach towards the water's edge where she would sit on the same stone, and look out across the ocean, as if waiting for something or someone. Then their eyes would meet, and they would just stay there like that for what felt like an eternity, before she would get up and leave.

Every time it felt like she was willing him to come ashore, as she watched him watching her, but what could he do? He could not approach the shore, the water was too shallow, so instead they continued this watching game, month after month. Kief felt there had become a silent connection between them.

Today, he watched as she appeared, regular as clockwork. But, immediately something was different today. She didn't stop to remove her shoes and adjust to the feel of the sand. Instead she strode out with, what appeared to Kief to be, a steadfast determination.

Passing her usual rocky seat, she continued walking into the water, deeper and deeper. As it reached her chin, Kief felt a sense of urgency seeping through him. He lowered himself from the rocks and sank into the water, careful not to lose sight of her.

As she vanished beneath the waves Kief dove down to keep her in view as he swam towards her. His underwater vision helped him to search her out quickly. She was just stood there, as if waiting for the ocean to carry her away.

Kief could see her eyes were open, they must be stinging with the heavy salt. As he drew closer, he could see much more in her eyes, a history of sadness, a hint of confusion as she watched him approach, but more, an intense longing, as if this was what she had hoped for.

He reached out to her, pulled her into his arms, and covered her lips with his mouth. Providing life air for her, to prevent her from drowning. He knew that in doing this something else would also occur, the air he breathed was not like that of land walkers, she could never return now. She sank against him and he could feel relief washing from her as she opened her mouth to his. Did she know? he pondered as he took her into the ocean, maintaining the mouth to mouth contact with her as he guided her swimming.

They reached his home just as he felt her go limp in his arms. The slumber would hold her now until the change was complete. He made her comfortable upon a coral bed, gently removing the clothing she would no longer require, and watched as the transformation began.

Webbing gradually crept between her toes, that would no longer feel the sand. Her legs, that would no longer walk along the beach, became coated in blue and silver speckled scales. Gills, that would enable her to breathe split out from her neck. She was already beautiful before, but now she was the most beautiful thing he had ever seen.

Later, she opened her eyes and smiled at him. Her hand reached down to touch her tail as she realised what she had become. Unsteadily she swam towards him and embraced him. It was then he discovered, though no words were spoken, that it was him she had been searching for, waiting for all along to come and take her away. She gave up life on land to be with him, under the sea for eternity.

21- NO PLACE LIKE HOME

A dark figure huddled against the wall, pulling the bin bags close to shelter from the coldness of the night.

Grimy hands cupped together in front of her face as she blew into them, hoping to reinstate some sensation other than the bone-deep, icy chill they now held. It made little difference as her frigid breath puffed out like smoke.

Painful emptiness in the pit of her stomach groaned out as she tried to wrap herself tightly in the flimsy coat that offered little comfort.

Resting her head against the wooden fence that ran at a right angle from the wall, it was warmer than the bricks at her other side, she felt as secure as she could be on the streets. Setting in for the night, sleep came quickly, but lightly, ready to awaken and move on in a hurry if need be.

****

He looked on waiting until he felt certain she was deep enough to make his move. It took some time to satisfy him as she seemed fitful in her slumber. He could sense that even in sleep she was ready to pounce and run like a frightened cat at the slightest disturbance.

This would be difficult.

Finally, a stillness came over her and he knew she was as immersed as she could be. Now was his chance.

Creeping slowly forward, taking care not to knock the bags around her, which would surely awaken her, he reached down and covered her nose and mouth. Once he was sure, he moved the bags and gently lifted her slight figure from its resting place and carried her away.

****

Eyes still heavy with sleep, she rolled over, softness surrounding her she leapt up with a start, panic consuming her – – this wasn't where she'd fallen asleep.

Eyes open, the familiarity of the room instantly struck a chord which sent a pang of fear and guilt cursing through her entire being.

Without looking she knew what she would see if she turned to her right, tears began to trickle down as she turned to face his still sleeping form.

He had found her.

****

He stirred as her movement roused him. Reaching out a hand to brush her matted hair off her wet cheeks, he smiled.

'Welcome home, darling, I missed you so much. You have no idea how hard it was to find you. Let me get you some breakfast and your medication. Then we can get you cleaned up. I can see we will have to be much more careful with you from now on. We don't want the doctors to put you back in the institute now do we? This running off must stop. I have the lock fitters coming shortly. I'll keep you safe from now on.'

****

Wiping away the tears she knew it was over. She would never escape again, this madman believed she was his wife and soon she would be doped up to the eyeballs again, trapped in his crazy world. Words would not form on her lips to protest, not that they had made any difference in the past – – he believed her to be the mad one. So much so that now, not for the first time, she began to wonder which of them was insane.

Either way it didn't matter. She was home.

22. POEM – FINGER ON THE TRIGGER

It flicked the switch
The trip-wire twitched
On a loaded gun …

It happened a few weeks ago
I don't want to talk about it
You don't want to know

You wouldn't believe me anyway …

I'm managing emotions
Camouflaging situations
A chameleon guise again …

Stories have been told
Different but the same
The truth won't unfold

This is my life, not a game …

23. DIALOGUE

'How was college today?'

Louise grunted, 'All right'

'That it? Why don't you talk to me anymore?'

Mary walked across the room and picked up the remote control.

'Don't, Mum, I'm watching this.'

'The news is on shortly and you haven't answered me yet.'

'You spend all day writing the news, why do you have to come home and watch it too? And I'm talking now aren't I?'

Mary sighed. 'Okay so tell me about your day, what did you do?'

'The usual, classes, hung out, nothing special.'

'Hmm, that's a start I guess.' Mary glanced at the TV, an image of cows in a milking barn was showing. 'Why are you watching a programme about a farmyard?'

'For my assignment.'

Mary sat next to Louise who is sprawled out on the reclining seat of the sofa, laptop at her side, can of coke in her hand.

'An assignment about farmyards on an IT course, how does that work?'

'This is the most advanced farm in the country, Mum, look at all that equipment, the whole thing is virtually run by computers.' Louise's eyes lit up as she spoke. 'The automation of so many processes that people used to have to do manually, it's awesome!'

'How do they manage that?'

'Well, it's all about the programming, the right command code and you can almost make the machines do anything. The next stage is introducing self-learning, so the robotic elements can correct their own mistakes, artificial intelligence … ' Louise was on a roll now, there would be no stopping her, all that was needed was to find a topic that interests her and the conversation just flows…

24. NOT FOR THE FEINT-HEARTED

The cool steel slides along like blades on ice, leaving a feint but growing red streak in its wake. She lifted, moved it down about a centimetre and felt a rush of adrenaline as it pierced again, a little deeper this time.

She took a deep breath as the pleasure kicked in where pain should have been, heart pounding ferociously as the deeper ooze of red welled, then followed the path of the steel, quickly surpassing it like a flooding river. Then, as a river tumbles over a cliff to become a waterfall, the scarlet stream flowed over the edge, splashing a perfect circle onto the brilliant whiteness below, puddling instantly.

Placing the steel aside she brought her mouth to catch the ebbing flow before it stopped. Looking at her handiwork, without the barest glimmer of regret, she turned to begin the clear up. A square of kitchen roll pressed lightly against the stemming streams, quickly soaked and stuck in place, another absorbs the blotch on the white side

Rolling down her sleeve to cover the tissue, a single tear tickles her cheek, and she wipes it away – it is meaningless. She retrieves the abandoned blade and runs the taps and wipes it clean of the evidence and returns it to the block amongst her other tools of self-injury – then returns to her chores before the household awakes, and another ordinary day begins …

25. STONES

'I have to go soon'

'I know, I know,' Sam sighed as he rolled his foot over the slippery, dark pebbles. The sunrise was beginning to creep from behind the clouds that hung moodily above the old castle.

Sam sat down on the pebble beach to wait for the tide to slip out further revealing the crossing to the small island the castle stood upon just off the shore.

'There's never enough time,' Sam whispered sulkily, his brow knit into a frown.

'Time is what you make of it,' his father's voice soothed the frown.

'I don't know about that.'

'You race through life to quick, son, slow down and enjoy the moment. Look at the beauty around you, even now.'

Sam's gaze carried across the shimmering, sea drenched pebbles to the island that looked inviting and peaceful. The crumbling castle would eventually succumb to the sea. Eyes lifting upwards, he noticed the sunrise bringing an unusually brown hint to the sky and realised his father was right, he never looked at anything properly anymore.

'I'm sorry, Dad,' he said, 'I just wanted you to be proud of me, so I've always focused on working hard to be successful, but I realise now you were proud of me anyway.'

'Very proud, son, and I love you very much. Do you remember ours walks along the beach when you were young?'

A hint of a smile began to spread along Sam's face as he

remembered those times. The tales his father would tell. His father explaining how, eventually, due to the water eroding them away, the large pebbles that made up the beach would get smaller, but the process of transforming from a pebble beach to a sandy beach would be much longer than Sam's lifetime.

Sam picked up a smaller pebble and skimmed it out onto the receding wash that gently lapped the seaweed coated rocks.

'It's time …'

Sam pushed carefully against the slimy stones as he got to his feet. Yes, it was time the pathway was clear now. He picked up the jar which had been sat beside him and carefully walked towards the castle where he would spread his father's ashes.

26. POEM – CHANGING

She holds her head high and laughs
(her tears won't fall any more)

She puts on a pretty dress and dances
(her legs won't walk any more)

She raises her voice and sings
(her words won't speak any more)

She gives her body and loves
(her heart won't feel any more)

She parties hard and fast
(her life won't live any more)

But then when she expects it least ...

Her tears flow
(She has found release)

Her legs stride
(She has found strength)

Her words flow freely
(She has found courage)

Her heart beats
(She has found happiness)

Her life moves on
(She has found freedom)

Change is a choice, not an option, and only you can do it ...

27. FORBIDDEN

Time seemed to move slowly as Amanda felt herself gliding through the air, well not so much gliding but still …

Each tumble felt like it would be the last as the concrete of the steps connected with her body.

She heard screams, and clenched her eyes shut tight, unsure if the noise was coming from herself or someone else.

Terrified, yet peaceful at the same time, she waited for the inevitable.

It would stop then, the pain, the fear, would all be over, when she reached the bottom.

At last, there came an almighty crunch but Amanda didn't hear it, didn't feel it as her neck snapped against the second from last step. Her body crumpled in a heap at the bottom …

Blackness …

Slowly she flickered her eyes open. Was she dead? Not daring to move, she tried to focus her eyes. All she could see was glaring whiteness. A hospital?

Blackness …

Tom watched as the girl opened her eyes briefly then faded back into unconsciousness. He wondered how long she would continue to drift, it had been six weeks now.

Not once had she done anything more than open her eyes, look confused, then fade again.

Amazingly her body was healing well after the mess he had found her in.

40 steep, concrete steps and the girl had been a bloody, messed up pulp at the bottom.

Had she fallen from the top?

Part way down?

Was she pushed?

He had no idea. All he knew was there was no one else around when he found her and in these days emergency services were only available to those who could pay.

So, he did what he could by himself, grateful that he had once worked in a hospital before they privatised even the portering.

He wasn't a doctor, but he had seen enough to know not to move her immediately. He had carefully checked to see if she was alive, found a slow but steady pulse. Ripping up his T-shirt, he stemmed the bleeding where he could. From the position of her head it seemed likely she had broken her neck.

How could he get her away from here safely if her neck was broken?

He couldn't just leave her to die; although without medical care – which there was no hope of –he didn't know how she would have much chance of surviving anyway. And if she lived, would she be able to move again?

Tom knew he'd need help to move the girl safely, so he pulled his iPhone out and called the only person he knew would have any idea what to do, Claire. Before the Troubles, Claire had been a paramedic – what better person to help him? Shit, she even had her emergency response vehicle still so maybe she would have some kit that would help save the girl's life?

Blackness …

Opening her eyes again, this time Amanda could focus. She could tell from the sensations around her body that she had healed completely.

This was not good, she had chosen the remotest place she could find to try and destroy this body. What foolishness had led to it surviving, human bodies were supposed to be fragile, weak, easily disposed of.

Now she was trapped here in the body of this girl instead of returning to her world. Rage engulfed her, she would destroy them all for this, what would they call it? Compassion? How dare one of these beings heal this body – she wanted to get out of it so badly!

She sat up and saw a man working across from her, his back to her. Lips moving in unspoken words she made him turn and face her.

The destruction of Earth would begin with this man …

On seeing his face, she stopped her chant – could it be?

Destruction may have to be postponed for a while, there was something here that mattered more than returning home, and this man was the start of something big …

S. L. GRIGG

28. THANATOS

The Thanatos rocked as a deep, hollow sound, accompanied by a burst of light in the window, shocked Corion from his downtime. Alarms beeped and flashed on the control panel, indicating the ship had been involved in an impact. Corion, instantly alert, began pushing buttons to locate and treat any damage the ship had incurred. He groaned as the scanner showed something imbedded in the hull. Sauntering to the exit hatch of the foredeck, he paused, calculating if he should alert the Admiralis before retrieving the item. Determining that retrieval prior to conversation was more appropriate, he exited the ship.

Corion proceeded to walk along the exterior of the ship to the collision point, discovering a golden- coloured cuboid covered in sensors and instrumentation. Assessment determined the impairment was superficial, and removing the article would not cause further damage. Corion could easily repair what harm had been incurred without need for a return to the foredeck. Having patched the hole effectively, Corion returned to the ship with the item and went to inform the Admiralis.

Corion entered the cabin affecting a bow. 'Admiralis'

'What is it, Corion?'

'We've had a minor incident, Admiralis,' Corion explained. 'My apologies for not having prevented it. It occurred whilst I was on downtime, otherwise I would've ensured we avoided the collision.'

'Damage report?'

'Superficial. Repairs have already been completed, and the object is on the foredeck for your inspection.'

'Let's have a look then, shall we?'

The Admiralis unplugged himself from the charging station and followed Corion to the foredeck.

Scanning the object, the Admiralis expressed a high level of interest in its origins. Various words were imprinted on the object, notably GOES-12 and NASA, which were highlighted within the Admiralis' archive memory banks.

'Corion, scan the vicinity of this galaxy for carbon-based beings immediately. I suspect we may find something of interest in this region either for the collection, or better yet, the objective of our mission.'

'At once, Admiralis.' Corion returned to the control panel. 'There appears to be a number of other items of debris, like this, directly within the locality that the ship automatically corrected to avoid further collisions. This debris field had not been previously plotted on our navigational systems but has now been recorded to prevent incident should we venture into this region in the future. Approximately three hundred kilometres beyond this is a planetary body which does indeed have carbon-based beings. Over eight-point-seven million individual species have been identified—an impressive haul for the collection, and based on previous galaxy findings, the likelihood of discovering our intended target is eighty-percent greater than prior discoveries. The GOES-12 indicates the beings here have managed to leave their own atmosphere, and precaution is advised; other satellites are in orbit closer to the planet.'

'Understandable, Corion' the Admiralis concurred. 'In that case, we should disguise the ship in a style matching the GOES-12 and prepare to set down in a lesser populated area of the planet.'

29. PERFECTION

Hidden behind the curtain I carefully line up glass upon glass. Checking each one for imperfections as I place it on the gold and black striped cloth.

Starting at the centre of the board, the first glass positioned, perfectly calculated to the millimetre. 120 glasses on the first layer.

An extra buff, as needed, to enhance the shine, a glittering array is a must.

Once the base board is covered, in perfect symmetry I begin to add a layer of glasses on top of the first. The beginning of a slow, delicate, precise building process. Each glass must be placed with the middle of its base resting upon the small space between the glasses below.

All in all, 680 glasses are to be aligned in a triangular formation. My task is not a small one, the slightest bump and they will all come crashing down.

The Captain's Circle event is less than an hour away as I begin to add the twelfth of fifteen layers, now working from a precarious set up of ladders and boards surrounding the fountain.

I worry about the oafish porters and the high potential for them to destroy my work when they remove the equipment once I have completed the display.

Finally the last glass in place, the whole thing is for photographic effect more than anything, as such, the task of erecting the glass tower was made much more difficult by the necessity of having the first ten layers pre-filled halfway so as to not waste too much time (or look too barren for the pictures) when the Formal Evening begins and the ship guests arrive to pose with the Captain and pour some champagne into the fountain for that 'once in a lifetime' memory shot.

My work complete, I watch over as the platforms are cleared and the marble effect stand for the passengers is bought into place. Not a nudge occurs, and I finally breathe again, the stage is set, the Champagne Fountain is ready.

Perfection.

30. POEM – CRISIS

As I lay me down to sleep

I do not cry,

I do not weep,

I do not ask you my soul to keep …

I am vulnerable and weak

Your sympathy I do not seek

That would only make me meek …

This life is thin, this life is fake

I hope to die before I wake

Cause I've had as much as I can take …

31. A PORTRAIT IN FICTION

She stumbles and falls … she picks herself up, dusts herself off and continues ploughing forward. Steady determination but heavy heart and tear streaked face.

The road is littered with a myriad of unsurpassable objects, too big and heavy for her to move alone, but she is alone. So instead she picks a way through, climbing over, slipping under, squeezing between what she can where she can.

Encumbered with the weight of a thousand difficult days, the memories of hurt and loss.

Another bomb drops, she shelters from the fallout under a paper-thin shroud that offers little protection.

She weathers a storm bare skinned, the rain striking her like white-hot pokers carving deep into her soul.

And still she presses on, each trip adding another bruise or cut that will not heal. Nothing stops her, sometimes she is held back for a while by the intensity of the barriers and blockages intent on stopping her dead.

But not for long, and still the world continues to throw its worst at her. To drive her insane, cut her to a quivering wreck.

Many others would surrender, give in, stop. She wants to, often, to curl up and let it wash over her, consume her. It is all too much, all too often.

Yet she finds the strength from somewhere to battle on, the journey is a persistent nightmare filled with demons and devils. The angels get taken away, or are caged out of her reach. Rarely any help or support to guide her, comfort her or make her feel safe.

There is no time for recovery between incidents, the next is upon her like a wave of hornets before she even has time to process what occurred before.

Powered by some indescribable force like that of a superhero robot she overcomes the crashes again and again.

She stumbles and falls ... she picks herself up, dusts herself off, and continues ploughing forward. Steady determination but heavy heart and tear streaked face.

32. HIDDEN IN THE MIST

'Ship's log: There 3473 passengers and crew aboard the *Grand Horn* cruise ship, a sickness began to pass through a few members of the crew 11 hours ago and now it seems that I, Captain Evans, am the lone survivor of whatever is causing my passengers and crew to eat each other alive. We are due to arrive in England at 0430 hours tomorrow, less than 24 hours after the sickness began. I don't know what to do …'

The vessel slipped silently along with the tide. I peered out into the mist wondering how close to shore we were and what I would do once we got there.

Alone on the bridge, I thought about the passengers and crew below with a heavy heart. Whatever this sickness was that had overcome them and caused so much terror and bloodshed was not something I could unleash on the unsuspecting nation, but I had no way to let them know what I was bringing to their shore. All communications had long since been lost when I had to cut off all power to the cruise ship in a vain attempt to trap the hordes of grotesque creatures in the decks below.

I have been bitten by one of these sick people and I was gradually beginning to feel that the sickness is consuming me too.

I closed my eyes and stared at the blood redness I could see of my eyelids, hunger filled me. I felt myself slipping away.

Shaking myself hard, I opened my eyes, an intense desire for flesh nauseating me, was this why these monsters had taken to ripping chunks out of each other like cannibals?

The stench of death and decay was unbearable even up here in the relative safety away from those things. Occasionally, a scream could still be heard as they breached another of the few barricaded areas and defeated the living trapped there. I felt disgusted that there had been no way I could help save these people when I had clearly saved myself.

A break in the mist showed a cliff face extending towards the vessel.

We would soon be run aground on the rocks beneath. Then what would occur? Would we stay trapped in here to face the finality of death imprisoned on a luxury cruise liner and ultimately an ocean grave? Or would rescuers come to help only to unleash this evil on the land before us and themselves be overrun by the bloodthirsty creatures?

My mind fogged again and the smells that previously sickened me now enticed me. I was changing, I could feel it, my skin long since greying and looking like that of the creatures I had seen mutiny my vessel.

Consciousness is fading.

A light shone from within the mist, it must be the lighthouse warning of the cliffs and rocks that I had no way to avoid.

An urge to join my fellow travellers surged through me and I reached out to the controls on the bridge panels, flicking the switch that would return power to the ship with weak trembling hands.

I needed to feed.

With what remnants of my humanity held, I moved along the controls enabling doors to open, lifts to work, and inevitably giving freedom to the captive crowds below. I dropped anchor and released the external doors that would allow us to spill out from the ship, into the mist and eventually onto the land ahead.

When I could no longer focus, I walked out of the bridge into a throng of stumbling writhing bodies, our only collective thought to feed, consume flesh and blood.

We spilled out of the ship, crashing into the water and rocks, picking ourselves up broken and battered, we moved forwards in an ungainly mass, walking under the water until we surfaced closer to the shore and proceeded up the beach the scent of life drawing us on …

We must feed …

33. TAXI TO ALL TIME

They were both giggling like school kids as they stumbled into the taxi, her not even letting go of his arm.

'I'm seriously smashed, we really shouldn't be doing this.' He smiled at her, the dimple in his cheek and twinkle in his eyes saying the opposite – how much he really wanted to do this.

She smiled back and kissed him on the cheek as he lent forward and told the taxi driver where to take them before leaning back and slipping an arm around her shoulders.

'Thanks for that,' he said to her with his usual level of fun sarcasm.

As normal, she didn't say a word. Whenever she was around him this way her intelligence faltered, and she was struck dumb, only able to giggle. She was besotted by him, many questioned if it was love or lust, she didn't know what it was, all she knew was that she wanted this more than anything every time she saw him.

She thought of how many times they had sneaked away in this manner, only for their indiscretions to be known regardless of neither of them uttering a word of it. The not so secret affair was constantly causing them trouble that both did not want. Nobody could deny the chemistry between them, it was obvious even at the times they avoided contact, merely catching each other's eye across the room. But, their body language and behaviour betrayed their attempts to play down their wanton yearning.

Of course, people asked why they didn't just get it together, and the excuses would rain down, littered with truthful realities from her being so much older than him, to family responsibilities and differences in lifestyles but in truth, there was nothing that could not be overcome with some effort from both sides – so why didn't they just do it?

The taxi slowed, he had spent the whole journey chatting away with the driver about nothing, while she had pondered about why they felt the need to hide their love. They paid the fare and stepped out.

'What are we doing?' he asked. That same hint of denial, suggesting he didn't want to be with her as if someone was listening and he had to keep up the act of there being nothing going on.

She just smiled and grabbed his arm again, which she had somehow let go of as they got out of the taxi. With a gentle tug, she led him down the path before them.

It was late, dark, and quiet. No one else was around, even the birds had gone to sleep, so the only sound once the taxi left was the distant traffic on the highway.

The pathway was intermittently lit by lampposts that were shaded by the trees.

A short way along the path, she stopped and pulled him through the bushes there into a dark clearing. Turning to face him, she was again entrapped by his long lashed, twilight blue eyes. They had stopped giggling now, an air of seriousness washing over them both.

He pulled her into a long, deep kiss and their hands began to wander, plucking away each other's clothes. The cold night air unfelt by their alcohol warmed bodies as they fell, embracing, on to the damp ground.

They enjoyed each other's bodies for a while with such passion and chemistry that they almost became one, before laying back and staring at the red hued, star speckled sky above through the branches of the still winter bare trees.

Eventually, she rolled over and with her arms folded on his chest she stared at the beauty of his face, the longing within her not abating in the slightest. She wanted to bottle this moment and keep it forever. That messy, unkempt hair, that slender, petite body, those gentle, oil filthy hands. There wasn't an inch of his body that she found displeasing, the same of his witty, cocky arrogant nature that so wound up other people just endeared him to her.

His hands ran over her sweat moistened skin, the passion within them both still clearly not subsiding. There was so much she wanted to say but the words running through her head did not form into speech.

He gently hoisted her up, so their faces were aligned and kissed her again. Then playfully pushed her off him, so she rolled back over next to him.

Easing himself off the ground he started to retrieve his clothing and she followed suit, the giggles beginning to return now as they snuck glances at each other all the while.

Once clothed, they moved together again. She slipped her arms around his waist and pushed her hips into his, leaning back slightly with her upper body to ensure she had a full view of his face.

He looked at her now, differently, the most earnest look he had ever given her. The time for play was over.

It was time to go.

They both knew there was no other way, being together in this life, in this world wasn't an option for them.

Emerging from the bushes they walked hand in hand, silently, sadly.

Ahead of them the great old bridge loomed into view, almighty and doom ridden. This was it.

He helped her up onto the wall, then joined her as they stood there looking out at the expanse of the lake far beneath. There were no guarantees this would work, but the drop was such that it seemed likely and at 3.00 a.m. there was no one around to see them jump and mount a rescue operation.

As they kissed again, a tear slipped from her eye, he wiped it away with his thumb when he looked at her.

Hugging her to him deeply for a final time he told her that he did love her and would give anything for things to be different, so they could be together in this world. But, they both knew that wouldn't happen. So, it didn't change anything.

A final kiss and they unwrapped themselves from each other's caress.

Standing side-by-side, hand-in-hand. They looked at each other, quietly mouthing 1 ... 2 ... 3 ... and jumped ...

34. POEM – PROGRESS

The time comes to walk away from your past,

Head held high and smile on your face.

Knowing what you leave behind is only waste,

Was holding you back, has been replaced.

Bigger and better,

Bolder and brighter,

Stronger and wiser,

New people, new places,

And happiness you didn't know you could achieve.

So, do not cry and do not grieve,

That which is gone was meant to leave.

S. L. GRIGG

35. CASSIE (WRITTEN AGE 14)

Cassie was different, no one knew what it was but they didn't like it. She would sit in the corner looking at something concealed in her hand then suddenly she would look up and say something like, 'Marco Walker, don't go to the mall tonight, be it on your own head if you go and something happens.'

No one would understand what she meant but since 'it' happened they would all listen carefully to what she had to say …

Carl was the only one who knew the full details of what happened to Bungle Malone. He had been there, Cassie had warned Bungle, but he didn't listen; he wasn't going to miss the new Batman movie for anything, even saving his own life. But then he wasn't to know it would come true.

It was a Friday morning when it all started. Cassie was, as usual, minding her own business in the corner when a look of terror came over her face. Never had she seen such an awful thing as this. She warned Bungle that if he went to the movie on Saturday night then he would be in deadly danger. But Bungle was the 'knock' of the class and he wasn't going to let a weirdo order him about, or anyone else for that matter! He said, 'You're stupid, weirdo, if you think I'm being taken in by any of your dumb stories!'

He and Carl did go to the movies that Saturday. Carl was worried and said, 'Maybe we should go home, what if something does happen?'

Bungle wasn't pleased. 'Are you mad? Believe that weirdo if you want but even if you don't go to the movie, I am. I've waited ages to see this and I'm not going to miss it for some superstitious nonsense!'

They went into the cinema and sat on the back row, throwing popcorn at each other and the people in front. As the adverts ended, Carl darted out to get some more popcorn. The lights went down for the film to start.

Suddenly, there was a huge bang and crash. Some people screamed, scared, and rushed for the doors. All wondering what was going on. The lights came up and they calmed down a bit. Everyone could now see what had happened. The weight from the heavy rain the night before had made the old roof boards weak at the back of the hall. The roof had fallen in on the back row of seats, crushing Bungle beneath its weight.

Carl had been coming back to his seat and had seen the boards fall onto Bungle. He was sitting on the stairs, white as a ghost muttering, 'Why didn't he listen?'

Bungle was dead, Cassie had tried but wasn't able to stop it happening and she blamed herself. 'Why, why, why didn't I make sure he didn't go?'

Since Bungle's death, Carl and Cassie came to understand each other. Carl knew what it was that made Cassie seem weird. She was gifted, nothing else, just gifted. Cassie had the power to see into the future. She had a ring with a rare unknown gem in it; this was like her third eye; the eye with which she saw what would happen.

It wasn't Bungle's fault, and it wasn't Cassie's fault about what happened. It was an accident. But, Bungle should have listened; he had been warned.

So, if ever someone who seems weird warns you to watch out, beware, or not to do a certain thing, think carefully before you decide whether to disbelieve them, or you might end up like Bungle. They could save your life – if only you listen!

36. HOUSEWARMING

Clare burst out laughing as she tried to repeat the line she had messed up, but again it came out wrong.

'Trousers in pockets ...'

This caused her to crack up even more, her sides hurt she was laughing so hard. Then Jane pushed two marshmallows into her cheeks and, looking like a demented hamster, squeaked something inaudible at Clare making the laughter turn to tears. Clare's ribs felt like they would burst through her chest as a horrendous snort came out of her which made Jane almost choke on the marshmallows.

It couldn't possibly get any worse, for fun of course. What had started out as a small celebration had almost turned into a riot. Clare didn't know who half of the people were who had crammed into her small house and she had spent most of her house-warming night chasing round trying to prevent these strangers causing any serious damage.

Of course, getting progressively more drunk herself didn't help and she just couldn't be bothered to try and get them to leave, everyone was having so much fun and she loved it.

Eventually, people began slipping away and those that remained were sleeping noisily in drunken stupors and their own vomit. Clare had allowed herself to sleep lightly too, but awakened early hoping to start cleaning up as her uninvited guests rose and left. Upon waking, however, Clare realised she would need some heavy-duty cleaning products so she decided to pop off to the local supermarket and grab some, it shouldn't take more than ten minutes.

That was her biggest mistake, or possibly her great escape.

The queues in the supermarket were already massive and it took much longer than planned.

Clare could see smoke on the horizon as she waddled out of the supermarket with her heavy bags. The air tasted acrid and the need to empty her stomach of last night's alcohol threatened to delay her further, but she managed to push the sensation building in her throat away as she strolled towards home. The smoke was clearly sign of a large fire, although the direction didn't immediately provide any further clues and anyway, Clare was far too distracted with controlling the stomach contents and thoughts of cleaning to consider it any further.

It wasn't until reaching her street that it became apparent that her home was the source of the fire ...

Five people died in her home that morning and to make matters worse, Clare was the main suspect. Arson was suspected, and the police believed Clare had deliberately set fire to her home in retaliation against the gate-crashers and for an insurance pay-out. Clare couldn't believe it, but what could she do?

She told the truth about all that had happened, never the type to hide things. Of course, it had been annoying that strangers had entered her home and party, but surely if she was that bothered she would have called the police? And besides, she wouldn't, couldn't hurt anybody.

Clare sighed as her lawyer looked her up and down when she finished explaining the events of the night and morning to him. Did he even believe her? Clare wasn't sure of anything anymore. Her heart was breaking, she had lost everything in that fire, including her best friend. Who could she turn to now?

37. DUET

Cheers and a raucous applause fill the room as Max takes a bow, blowing kisses as he plays up to the audience.

The pub is heaving for a school night, as we call it. Thursday night, most of us have work tomorrow, but that doesn't stop us coming out once a month for the infamous karaoke night at The Sun. It's rumoured a previous performer was picked up by a scout from a recording company here, but details are vague and vary depending who's telling, probably not true.

I take a slug of my beer as John, the DJ, announces the next singer, Caroline, who will be singing 'Need you now' by Lady Antebellum.

Stuart nudges me, 'Isn't that meant to be a duet, Rob?' I nod, watching as a short, nervous-looking girl steps up to the mike. I've not seen this Caroline before and I can't take my eyes off her already, damn. She is visibly shaking as the music starts. Eyes wide with fear, her mousy brown hair in a poker straight bob brushes her shoulders. She looks like she came in straight from work, in her figure hugging pinstripe shift dress and mid-heeled smart shoes. She closes her eyes and begins to sway a little.

I hold my breath as she begins the first verse, I love this song, please don't ruin it, I think. Her voice is quiet but pitch perfect, a silence comes over the busy pub, as everyone turns to look at the source of this angelic voice.

'Louder, darling,' someone calls out, but she is lost in the music.

I am on my feet before I think. At the DJ booth I signal to John for the other mike. I can't let her do this duet alone, I need to step in before the chorus.

Just in time, I cross the dance floor towards her, and join in with the chorus. She opens her eyes and turns towards me. We are in perfect harmony, naturally. Neither of us needs the words on the screen, and she has stopped shaking. It is as though the rest of the room has melted away and just the two of us exist at this moment.

Her face is lit up with the most beautiful smile I have ever seen. As we come to the end of the song, we have moved together, eyes locked. I reach out and put my hand on her waist as the music fades. Drawing her close, the crowd cheering and whopping as I lean in and kiss her. This could be the start of something good.

38. LIZARD

Kate jumped at the hand on her should, dropping the binbag she was lifting out of the bin, its contents slipping over the kitchen floor. She span round, her elbow smashing into the box in Jack's hand, almost knocking that to the floor too.

'Hey, careful, clumsy boots, this is fragile!'

'Holy shit, Jack! Me be careful? What are you doing creeping up on me like that? Have you done the shopping?' Kate didn't take a breath as the words rushed out, frustration etched on her face. She observed no bags on the kitchen table. Eyebrows raised, she tilted her head to the left questioningly as she looked up at him.

'Yeah, yeah, it's in the boot. I'll go grab it in a sec, I just wanted to give you this first.' He held the box out to her.

'What is it?' she asked taking it from him, and placing it on the table with a frown.

'Just open it,' Jack's eyes glinted to match the grin that spread across his face.

He was like an excited child, Kate half expected him to begin jumping up and down. Pulling out a chair, Kate sat down wearily, not matching Jack's enthusiasm.

Inside the box was a lizard, unlike any she had seen before.

'What the … why?'

'I remembered how much you said you loved your gecko as a kid and thought you would like it?' It was Jack's turn to have a questioning look on his face.

'Where on earth did you get it from?'

'Well, actually I found it by the side of the road.' Kate's furrowed brow made him continue without her having to say a word. 'Yeah, so I had pulled over to take a leak, and it was just there, in the grass verge. So, I just grabbed it and it just let me, so I figured it's kinda friendly. I popped it in this shoe box you had left in the boot, then carried on to do the shopping—'

Kate interrupted, 'And where are we supposed to keep this thing?'

'Ahh, see I went into Pets at Home next door to the supermarket and got all the gear, terrarium the works!' Jack exclaimed. He lifted the lizard from the box and held it closer to Kate, who instinctively put out her hands to receive it.

Once the lizard was in her hands, she couldn't help but admire its scaly skin, cool to the touch and as it looked at her, she was in awe of its unusual eyes, almost cat-like compared to lizards she had seen before. It nuzzled her hand and its claws tickled her palm as it curled up and settled.

'See,' Jack said, 'It likes you already. I'll go and get the shopping in and we'll get him settled into his new home.'

Later, once the shopping had been put away and the terrarium was all set up. Jack sat admiring his find, whilst Kate was busying herself on the laptop.

'I can't find any lizards even remotely like this thing,' she explained to Jack. 'The only thing that looks anything like it is movie dragons.' She laughed at the notion, but Jack was unresponsive. She looked up, 'Jack did you hear me?'

Turning to see why Jack was so quiet she was shocked by what he was watching in the terrarium. The lizard appeared to be sneezing, but with each tip of its head as it blew out a sneeze a small puff of smoke puffed from its nostrils.

Kate jumped to her feet, grabbed hold of Jack's arm, and gave a little squeal of excitement.

'Oh my god, Jack! You brought home a dragon, an honest to god, non-existent, real- life dragon! Damn, we are gonna be rich! Famous and rich! You are the most amazing boyfriend in the world!'

39. POEM – SKY

When it's dark and quite
While my World sleeps
I sit and stare
Feel the magic in the air

The sky at night
A true delight
Moodily cloud covered
Or sparkling clear

I love to see the stars that shine
Constellations I can barely name
And the moon
Waxing, waning, crescent or full

The sky at night
A true delight
Peaceful and free
Alone with just me

The colours behold me
Blues of every shade
Sapphire and twilight
Prussian and midnight

Deep purple to maroon
All gone too soon
As dawn creeps in
Bringing new light

The darkness fades
Stars hide away
Birds begin to sing
New light on everything

40. HIDE AND SEEK

'I think we lost her, Larry'

The gruff whisper with which John spoke caused Larry to tense up and grimace, clenching his fists he swung round, whispering a sharp response. 'Fer fuck's sake, John, keep yer' voice down.' Shaking his head in disbelief, Larry props his rifle against his shoulder as he surveys the area.

'Sorry, Larry,' John attempts to speak at a lower volume and it really isn't much better. Drawing a finger and thumb across his lips as though to zip them shut, he lumbers after Larry, his heavy gait further causing Larry to cringe at the noise he makes.

After a few minutes wondering blindly through the darkened woods, Larry shakes his head to himself, *think of the money Larry, just think of the money.*

Larry grabs John by the arm and stretches up to whisper in the taller man's ear, 'Let's get back t'car, I think I can guess where she'll end up from 'ere. Thomas will get us there in no time.'

Stopping in front of a fallen tree, John simply nods, but his brow is furrowed as though he doesn't really understand as he follows Larry back to the Thomas and the car.

As the two men walk away a face peeks out from under the fallen tree.

1.

The New Year celebrations ended a little over 24 hours ago, leaving 2016 resigned to the history books.

I am driving back to university in Worcester after spending Christmas with the family in Aberystwyth. Mum and Dad retired to there, leaving our home town of Birmingham the year after I left home to start university. It's lucky for some, hey. Their youngest daughter, I'm in the final year of a biomedical science degree and trying to decide where I will go after. Maybe if I can get a full-time laboratory job somewhere, that will help determine my location. In the meantime, Christmas with the family, always a chore to be endured, but hey they're family, it's worth it, right? Still, I'm glad to be heading home. No more bickering like children with my two older sisters and chasing around after Tammy and Jake, my oldest sister, Kate's, two kids, who, despite how much I love them, I just could not handle another for another day!

The winter countryside is a lush patchwork of frosted greens and browns by day. I love the wide-open spaces, the lack of people, rush and chaos of cities. There's nothing I can compare with time spent inhaling fresh, unpolluted air; well unless you pass a freshly manure covered, or rapeseed field. At night, though, the A44 is unlit in many sections on the route through Herefordshire. Other than my headlights, a sprinkling of stars and the quarter moon shining in the cloudless sky are the only illumination. Another bitter cold, winter night; I'm sure there will be a heavy frost in the morning. My dashboard shows it's minus 2, and we've not reached the coldest part of the night. Thankfully I have the heating up full blast, so I barely notice how cold it is. I don't even have my coat on. I smile, glad I won't have to defrost the car in the morning; rather I will just be curling up under my duvet having reached the dorms. Gliding along at 60 mph, I am in my element.

Some people would think it's crazy, a young woman driving alone at night. It's not like I need to be back at uni for a few days yet. I could easily have waited until the morning. But I like driving at night, the solitary, peace; the lack of other traffic. And truth be told, other than the kids driving me crazy, I just want to get back to my girlfriend, Kirsty. I've yet to find the courage to tell my folks about her.

I turn the radio up, cheesy old classics. Gene Pitney and Marc Almond, I do believe, I can't quite recall the song title, though. I sing along, well the words I know at least ... Nodding my head and drumming my fingers on the wheel in time to the music. A yawn breaks through, distorting my already dire attempt to hold a tune. I should consider taking a break soon.

Despite the chill outside, I open the window a crack. It lets in the only sound from outside, my car's wheels on the road. A gush of icy air hits me. I pull a cigarette from the pack I keep in the coffee cup slot in the centre console. Keeping one hand on the wheel, I manoeuvre the cigarette from pack to mouth, pull my lighter from the packet and click, click, until the flame bursts forth. A few chuffs and I'm lit. I push the lighter into my jeans pocket. Smoking is something I really should stop but it sure helps you stay awake when driving long distances, although, it certainly does let the chill in having the window open. I finish as quickly as I can, so I can close the window and get the warmth back. Brrr, I shiver, but it's not long before the car is warm again.

Another glance at the dashboard reaffirms the need to stop. I'm running low on fuel, hopefully there will be a garage soon. The sat nav isn't showing anything nearby and despite the empty roads, I don't think it will be worth the risk to try and fiddle with it whilst I drive to find one. I probably should have filled up before I left Mum and Dad's, but I thought 100 miles in the tank would just about cover it. The temperature is now 3 degrees above zero. A light fog begins to descend with the rising temperature, so much for the lovely, clear skies.

Turning my attention back to the radio, the pre-recorded host confirms they are currently counting down the top 10 hits of 1989, at number three, 'Eternal Flame' by The Bangles. Mum would have a fit if she caught me calling these cheesy old classics, ha!

'Jess!' she would holler, 'These tunes aren't even 30 years old yet. You want cheesy old classics you need to be thinking of things at least 40-50 years old, like your gran would have listened to; or rather forced me to listen to when I was growing up!'

'Mom, 80s and 90s classics are the best. I'm not criticising; just telling it like it is,' I would reply with a laugh.

Dad, on the other hand, would be chiding me for my driving skills, with his tips to conserve fuel. Those would be quite handy right now I think as the fuel light glows red and the annoying beep, beep highlights I have less than 30 miles to empty. I didn't factor in that having the heating on full blast would use more fuel, d'oh! Still no tell-tale symbols on the sat nav to indicate a petrol station in the vicinity. I might have to come off the highway and head towards the next town to see if I can find somewhere to fill up.

Within minutes of the rise in temperature the fog becomes so dense it's like a dirty, grey blanket smothering the Earth. Worse than pitch-black. A murky gloom throwing thick billows of smoke that roll through the headlights making me flinch as though they will impact. Even with my fog lights on, visibility has dropped to 20 yards or less, I can barely see past the bonnet. The lights cast a muddy brown, beige, glow in the mist, just reflecting at me rather than lighting the way ahead. They are virtually useless. I slow to around 20 mph, as I wouldn't be able to see if there was a bend in the road, or anything else for that matter. I'm using the dim view of the kerb as a guide to stay on the road and avoid ending up in some ditch. Clenching the steering wheel, body rigid, knuckles white, I realise I'm holding my breath. Driving in the dark I like, but not this. I grit my teeth so hard they hurt. I turn the radio off needing every ounce of concentration and all my senses. Opening the window a touch, I can hear the reassuring sound of the road. Heart in throat, I swallow hard. This is scary shit. I hope the fog lifts soon. It's crushing.

After what feels like an eternity of driving through hell, the fog begins to thin, and a fine mist of rain replaces it. There are still patches of haziness but the further I go, the less they become, and the heavier the rain gets. The swoosh of the wipers provides a comforting rhythm and I feel the tension begin to ease out of me and then the temperature begins to drop again as the rain too stops. I switch the radio back on for some company.

I continue, but fatigue is beginning to grind on me and I'm getting anxious about the fact I don't have enough fuel to make it home. And after that scary run through the fog, I just want to get home fast now. As the news comes on the radio indicating it's now 3.00 a.m. I flick over to the CD player, Coldplay's 'Fix You' takes its place, my favourite track. I haven't seen another vehicle in ages. While I'm sure there must be plenty of farms around here, it's impossible to see anything other than black expanses of fields when there is a gap in the roadside bushes.

Eventually I feel the car begin to stutter. I manage to pull over into a lay-by just before it finally grinds to a halt. As the car dies, I'm almost blinded by the headlights of an oncoming vehicle. What appears to be a classic American style hearse passes slowly on the other side of the road. I watch in admiration. As much as I adore my little red Fiesta that I saved up hard to get from my measly wages as a part-time medical laboratory assistant, my dream car would be one of those, a Cadillac Deville Hearse. When it is almost too late I consider jumping out and waving it down for help, but then I remember I have my phone. It might be late but I'm sure there's someone I can call. Good thing I have the phone as it's a bit far off to notice me if I jumped out now. Foolishly, I don't have any breakdown cover so there's no point ringing the AA. Actually, I think, it's a bit creepy, a hearse driving around at this time of night, not like there's any funerals to go to. A shiver runs down my spine and I'm glad I didn't act on instinct and wave it down. Removing my seatbelt and fishing my bag out from the footwell of the passenger seat to find my phone, I soon discover there is no signal. Fat lot of good my phone is now.

Weighing up my options, I decide it will be better, and safer, to lock the car and try to get some sleep. Walking around country roads, in the cold and dark, with no idea how far the nearest garage is certainly doesn't seem like a good idea to me. Better to wait until it gets light, so I can at least see where I'm going. The last town I recall seeing on the sat nav was Walton, so if memory serves the next one will be Kington. Although I'm not sure which will be closer? I guess it would be better to head to Kington as I know I didn't see any signs for petrol stations when I was near Walton. It would be funny, if it wasn't so cliché. Typical horror story setup, lone female breaks down in the middle of nowhere, hahaha, humph. No need for thoughts like that, I've had enough scares for one night!

I reach into the backseat to grab my thick, winter coat. With the car not running it's quickly getting cold in here. Better wrap up, hat and scarf too. Then I recline the driver's seat, check the doors are locked and lay back to have a nap while I wait for the sun to come up in about, oh crap, four hours or more …

2.

The sound of a car pulling up on the gravel lay-by wakes me. I open my eyes and sit up. What appears to be the hearse I saw earlier is pulled in front of me, bonnet to bonnet. As I rub my eyes, I can just make out someone sitting behind the steering wheel opposite me. The main beams come on, blinding me. I squint and try to peer round the lights. I can just about make out a figure getting out of the passenger side. No that's wrong; it's the driver's side, because I saw the steering wheel. I must have been right about it being a classic American hearse. They must have been coming back, saw me and stopped to see if I need help, I think. No need to blind me though.

I straighten up my seat as the figure moves and stops at my door. It has a massive, hulking body. Very tall too, I can't see the head or face. He tries the door, but it's locked. Just as I am about to wind down my window to speak to him I catch a glimpse of something. The headlights catch on something metallic. The person stood by my door is holding something with a longish handle and metal at the end. Hammer? Axe? I don't know but whatever it is I don't feel like they have stopped to help. A tremble of fear seeps through me.

As the individual raises the object I scurry across to the passenger seat. Just in the nick of time. The window smashes as the hammer, I can see now what it is, crashes through it. I fumble for the handle and literally fall out of the passenger side of my car. I drag myself up and dive for the bushes, scrambling as thorns tear at my skin. Blood trickles down my cheek.

The bushes open into what seems to be a grassy field, with a black line of trees in the near distance. I make a dash for the trees as I hear the attacker following me through the bushes. I daren't look back. In the gloom of the late hour it is almost impossible to see anything other than shadowy shapes. I just run, which is a feat. Why did I have to be so unfit? 21, 5 feet four inches tall, and a size 14, weighing in at over 11 stone, smoking isn't the only thing I need to sort out. I enjoy chocolate and fast food far too much for an impoverished student. Not that my vices are important right now. I'm running for my life. Or at least it feels like it.

Tripping on a hole in the grass, I twist my ankle slightly. I peek over my shoulder as I pick myself up. The figure is striding towards me. With his lofty gait, it's likely he'll catch up with me before long. Is that a second figure there, back closer to the bushes? Ahh, geez if there's two of them I'm even more screwed than I already thought I was! I run again as fast as I can manage, more of a hobble really now my ankle is hurting. A shrill whistle pierces the air coming from the direction I have just run from, probably one of them signalling to the other? It can't be far, but it feels like forever before I reach the tree line.

Ducking behind the first tree I reach I risk a glance back. I can't see the lead stranger coming, but that doesn't mean he isn't there. Just run, goddamn it, run!

Under the cover of the trees, I consider that how dark it seemed before, pales compared to the vast nothingness now. Pitch-black under bare, skeletal trees, not even the moonlight can break through despite the lack of a leafy canopy. How will I ever find my way to help here?

As I scramble on, I am acutely aware of the racket my own footsteps make as I crunch through the undergrowth and slightly frosted, dry, decaying leaves. My heart is pounding in my chest and I feel certain you could hear that for miles around too. I need to move noiselessly, like that is possible, I'm not a ninja. Every step gives away my position. Everything else is silent on this mid-winter night, not a sound of any living thing. This at least gives me some comfort. Surely, I would hear the predators if they are coming? They might even give their location away by using a torch if they have one. I know I would be glad of one right now, but then it would make me easy to find. Breathing heavily, the puffs of vapour pouring from my nose and mouth must surely be another beacon catching in tiny strands of moonlight to indicate my location.

Slowing down to reduce the amount of noise I am making seems like a good idea. Although my fight or flight reaction has me on full flight alert. A little sanity tells me stealth may be beneficial over speed here. I need to evade detection. If only I didn't have to breath as well.

One thing is certain, I am so glad I had put on my coat to sleep. It is so bitter out here I'd certainly be suffering hypothermia soon if it wasn't for the adrenaline helping to keep me from freezing.

Besides the omnipresent danger this is oddly reminiscent of childhood games of hide and seek with my sisters.

'Quick, Jessica, this way,' Kate would whisper as Sarah, face pressed against the old oak tree in the small woodland behind our house counted 'Seven, eight, nine …' We would run and try to find a hiding place.

'I'm coming!' Sarah would call out and I would give a little shriek of panic, giving away where I was hiding.

Shrieking would not be a clever idea now.

'Shh, Jess. You're meant to be quiet when you're hiding,' I can hear Kate admonish. *Thanks, Kate*, I think to myself as I continue to sneak along, wishing she were here to guide me now.

Just as I think, maybe they didn't follow me into the woods, I hear the same distinctive crunching that I was making, somewhere behind me. Not too close, but not so far away that he wouldn't quickly catch me up. It's so hard to keep moving forward quietly, dodging protruding undergrowth, creeping round trees and making sure I don't accidentally double back straight towards the strangers. Touch alone guides me as I feel me way round the gnarled bark of trees. Although my eyes have adjusted to the darkness, there is nothing much to see, touch is far more useful. All the while the pain in my ankle throbs, further slowing my progress, I'm sure I must have sprained it.

I stumble on the branch of a fallen tree. As I trip, I hear voices but can't make out what they are saying. The fallen tree has a ditch beneath it, and I roll into the gap to hide as the voices come closer. I make out the words, *lost her,* from the first voice, and the second seems to be telling them to shut up. I don't hear what else is said, but I get the feeling they are almost above me. I hold my breath, and imagine someone standing on the other side of the fallen tree. Then it sounds as though they are moving away. I wait, and listen carefully for a few seconds, then spotting an opening under the tree, I peek out, and watch two figures walking away from where I am hidden. I breath a silent cry of relief, and after waiting a few minutes to be sure they don't come back this way, I carefully creep out from under the tree and start moving away from the direction the figures had gone.

I have no sense of direction. Even without being in some woods in the middle of nowhere. I wouldn't have a clue if I'm headed north, south, east, or west. All I know is I'm heading deeper into this veritable forest, away from the road and my car, away from danger?

In a small clearing. The faint moonlight reveals it is surrounded by more trees. I freeze. I don't want to cross where I will be clearly visible to my pursuers. My heart thumps in my chest. After a brief pause and panic, I dash back into the woods a few yards up from where I came out. Moving along, I keep the clear space to my right, so maybe if the creeps cross it I will see them before they see me.

Tucking my hands up into my sleeves away from the frigid air it feels like I have been limping through the woodland for ages. Every so often I think I hear the stalkers, but then I'm not sure, it could be a creature moving about instead. It could even just be my imagination.

As I think I'd really like to stop and rest, I notice through the shrubbery a denser, larger shape than the usual raft of tree trunks. Is it a building? I edge closer, cautiously.

I reach out and touch the structure before me, brick, not wood. It is definitely some kind of building. I look up, even though it is so dark I can't see anything properly, the slope of a roof is just about discernible. It seems to be a single storey structure. I decide it won't hurt to see if there could be somewhere to hide or maybe I can get help. A person, a phone, anything other than staying out here, never knowing if the people chasing me might catch up. So, I start to work my way around, hoping to find a window or door.

3.

As I carefully manoeuvre my way along the first wall I find that a small, boarded up window is the only thing on this side of the building. The front is more open and therefore requiring an even more cautious approach. Wooden steps I dare not tread on lead up from a small patch of what may once have been a garden to a rickety, worn veranda and the front door. There is a little more luminescence here due to the open space allowing moonlight to peak through. Here, too, I can see, rather than feel, boarded up windows. It certainly seems this place must be empty, abandoned, probably for some time. My hopes of help are diminishing rapidly as I take in the decrepit condition of the bungalow with my new-found vision.

Best not to linger in this exposed space. As I daren't risk trying the front door, for fear of crashing through the rotten wood, I work my way round the other side of the building. To my disappointment, there nothing on this side either. A final chance awaits me at the back of the property. Before I can turn the corner, I hear a noise. Crouching as low to the ground as I can get, with my back to the wall, I listen warily to try and work out what the noise was. I stiffen, lips trembling.

A badger lumbers slowly round from behind the building. Hand over my mouth I stifle a cry of relief. Holding my position, I hesitate until the badger is clear. Not wanting to startle it in case it gives me away or even, God forbid, attacks. I've no idea if those things do that or not but I'd rather not take the chance. They're much bigger than I thought. Once I feel satisfied it has moved far enough away and I can hear nothing else, I press on.

Staying low I poke my head round the final corner before sidling my body round. Like the front, it is a bit more open here, but there is also a further extension of the building. I realise, yes, the first wall had been much longer than the one I have just moved along, the building is in fact quite 'L' shaped. On the wall ahead I see a door. It appears slightly ajar. Keeping on my guard, I decide to try it.

The door opens into a garage. As my eyes adjust again to the hazy view I see twin shutter doors through which a vehicle would enter are to my left, and a door to the main building to my right. Junk, shelving, old car parts, and toolboxes litter around the edges. Enough room for a large car in the middle of the oil stained floor. I wonder briefly if there may be a roadway leading from the property beyond the garage doors. Uncertainty fills me. What should I do? Continue exploring the building, knowing a working landline is unlikely given the state of the place, or go back out and follow the road, if there is one?

'Better safe than sorry,' Dad would say, always one to err on the side of caution. Damn he will give me hell when he hears about what has happened tonight.

'I told you,' he would scold. 'You should wait till morning. It's not safe a girl driving alone at night, but no, you don't listen to Dad, do you?' And in this instance, I would have to admit he was right for once.

'What should I do, Dad?' I say under my breath, already knowing the answer.

No, it's still so dark, I'm lost enough. At least here I can hide and keep a bit warmer. Sleep is out of the question, despite being aware of how much I need it, the adrenaline pumping through me would make it impossible, even if I felt safe enough to try it. Loitering has already given the creep plenty of time to catch up, if I go back out now I could walk straight into him, them, were there two or was my mind just playing even more tricks on me? Regardless, one or two is irrelevant right now. Not getting caught by anyone is my priority. I must hide and wait for some light before making a dash for it. Who knows, he might have already given up, but surely, he wouldn't continue a pursuit in daylight when others might see him too?

As I reach for the handle of the back door I spot a candle on the nearest shelf of junk. Taking it as it might be helpful inside I thank my lucky stars that I put my lighter in my pocket earlier. At least I have one useful thing on me, otherwise my pockets are empty. Bag and phone discarded in the car, even my fags. I sigh quietly, what I wouldn't give for a smoke right now.

I find a kitchen on the other side of the door. As the door closes behind me, my heart begins to pound as again I am consumed by darkness. Of course, all the windows are boarded up, so no light can enter.

With sweaty palms, I attempt to light the candle. After a few failed clicks, the lighter sends up a hot flame stinging my eyes with the sudden brightness. Blinking back spots, I light the candle and secure my lighter back in my pocket. I cup the flame with one hand to reduce its glare and take in my surroundings. There's not much to see, a simple understated compact kitchen area. Narrow but, I presume, as long as the back of the house. Cooker, 50's style fridge and lots of dust. However, it is also clear from smoother patches on some work surfaces that someone has been using this place recently, even if not much. It makes my skin crawl. Worse is the smell. I didn't notice at first probably due to my nose being practically frozen. I don't know what death smells like, but if I had to describe it this putrid scent, death would be it. I pray it is just some animal that got trapped inside and died and that the smell is not something more sinister.

There is no door in the wall from the petite kitchen to the next room. Again, it is a small room, shorter than the kitchen, but squarer. A large rug with a dark centre, whether it is naturally that way or stains I cannot tell, takes up most of the space. A sofa, half-hidden under filthy plastic, a small arm chair, uncovered, and a dining table with two chairs fill the rest of the room. No TV and plenty more dust tickling my nostrils. So far there doesn't appear to be anywhere I could hide in here. Anyone following me in would find me in no time. There is a door the other end of the room almost diagonally from me across the mat.

As I walk across the rug a large creaking sound echoes through the room. The floor gives way beneath me and I crash down …

4.

I open my eyes, are they open? It's too dark to tell. My head is pounding. Everything hurts. For a second I think I was just having a nightmare, but then I realise it is real. I fell. I must have been knocked out. How long for? Oh, my god if the stranger hasn't found me already; I'm a sitting duck now. I try to sit up; I can't put weight on my left arm. It gives way as I try to lift myself. A dead weight, I think it is more likely dislocated than broken, but still useless right now. The right takes the strain alone and I push and roll myself to a seated position, the rubble scraping and squeaking as I move. A sticky dampness trickles down my forehead, blood? Tentatively I feel my head and find a very tender spot where there is a gash, it probably feels bigger than it is.

Broken floorboards dig into me. I'm no doctor, but I don't think I have sustained any serious injuries from my fall. My ankle hurts even more than before and of course there's my arm and the cut on my head, but otherwise I think I will just have some nasty bruises. It would help if I could see if there was any more blood. Shit, the candle. Palpitations tremble through my chest and I catch my breath. I guess as there isn't any fire it must have gone out as I fell, but where is it?

Furtively I feel around the broken planks. There it is thankfully. I retrieve the candle and rest it on my thigh whilst I dig out the lighter, unsure how I will manage to light the candle one handed. I settle on standing it between my knees and once it is lit and the lighter back in my pocket I take it with my good hand. After checking myself over and finding no obvious sign of blood loss I hold it up to get a look at my new surroundings.

Bile rises as I observe the grotesque décor of the basement. That explains the smell from earlier, which now I think of it, is back, stronger than ever unsurprisingly. There is a nauseating stench of rot with an undertone of bleach and chemicals. The carcasses of numerous animals hang to one side. Jars full of organs line a shelving rack to the other side. The flame weaves and flickers, making the disgusting site even more macabre. In front of me is a workbench, stained with the blood and gore of whatever gross activities have been undertaken here and some large plastic barrels around it. Are those hospital boxes? White, insulated type boxes are stacked in a pile on the other side of the workbench, there is red writing on them that I can't make out from over here without my glasses, but I highly suspect it says Human Organ. I feel sick to my stomach. Are they harvesting organs for the black market or something, is that what they want with me? I must get out of here.

In the far corner, I spot a flight of stairs that must lead back up to the ground floor level. Carefully, I rise to my feet. Unsteady. As I walk over towards the stairs I hear movement above me. Someone or something is in the building. In the candlelight, I quickly try to find something I could use as a weapon. It's a waste of time. Whoever is responsible for all this horror must be some kind of neat-freak as well as a full-on freak! There are locked boxes on the worktop behind the workbench. All the tools of this terrible trade must be contained within them. Not so much as a single scalpel is out on view.

Going up the stairs would likely take me straight into the waiting arms of whoever is up there, but it is only a matter of time before they come down here to find out who has left a hole in the middle of their lounge! But there is nowhere to hide, except under the stairs themselves. Not much of a hiding space, but there are at least boxes. It's a slim chance, but maybe luck will be on my side. The owner may think it was just a badger that fell through and has since managed to get out. Better yet, they won't be the same person that was pursuing me. If they are the same they will certainly realise it must have been me, and not give up looking until I am found. Then what will they do with me?

Extinguishing the candle, I squeeze, bottom first in between the boxes, and shuffle back to the wall. Using my working arm, I feel my way back, touching something soft but hard as I reach the point where the floor meets the wall. I swallow down a little stomach acid that has risen to burn my throat at the thought of what I might just have touched. With my knees pulled up to my chest, good arm wrapped around my legs, and useless arm resting over the top I await my fate.

5.

From somewhere above me, I hear the faint sound of voices. I can't make out what is being said but after what sounds like heated discussion, footsteps head off in different directions. A door slams in the distance, but closer, another opens. Light floods into the basement as someone hits the light switch and begins to descend the stairs. Again, I am holding my breath, how many times is that in one night?

Dust and grime falls onto my head as the stairs bounce with the weight of the person coming down. I resist the urge to sneeze and hope it doesn't just happen and give away my hiding place.

Halfway down, the person stops, I glance up trying not to move too much. Can they see me down here from the gaps in the slated staircase?

The man stops again when he reaches the bottom, probably taking in the mess from where I fell through the floor.

From where I'm sitting I can't see much as he moves across the room. The occasional glimpse of his massive bulk reminds of Hafþór Júlíus Björnsson, 'The Mountain' from *Game of Thrones*, or one of the competitors from *World's Strongest Man*, as he is better known to me. Monstrously big, the sight of someone that big is enough to fill you with terror, even if you weren't already frightened for your life! It seems highly probable this is the same person who smashed my car window. It would be a huge coincidence that another person who was that big was in such proximity. It's not like we are in the land of the giants.

Metallic sounds echo, clinking together or against the wooden workbenches. I presume he is opening boxes and removing tools or weapons. I think I'm going to wet myself, I don't know how much longer I can sit here wondering what will happen next, I think as a shadow is cast over the gap between the boxes. Shit. I gasp.

A hand knocks away the front most boxes and grabs my ankle. I am pulled like a ragdoll. Try as I might to kick out and struggle, it is in vain. A horrific scream fills the silence, and it takes me a moment to realise that tortured noise is coming from me.

My already bruised back smacks onto the floor as I am ripped from my hiding place, boxes tumbling onto me. I reach out with my good hand to find something to grab onto, rolling over onto my front as I am dragged along.

'No, no, no!' The only words I can form tumble out in agonising squawks, as my nails scrap the floor.

In the jumble of stuff disturbed from the falling boxes, my hand grazes against something just as my lower body begins to rise from having been dragged out enough for a hand to grab my other leg closer to the knee. I grab hold of the object and establish it is a large, heavy, metal tool, maybe a wrench.

The man carries me with ease, no amount of wriggling making any difference in his vice like grip. I am thrown awkwardly as the hand on my ankle releases quickly securing a grasp of my limp arm sending shockwaves of pain running through me and threatening to make me pass out. It takes every ounce of strength to stay with it, but a further scream rises in a crescendo of misery.

I kick my loose leg wildly, not hitting home as I flail about like a tiny child being given an unwanted leg and a wing by a nasty older sibling.

He swings me upwards again and flops me down onto the workbench, putting an end to my bellows as the breath is knocked out of me briefly. As he comes into view properly for the first time, I am surprised by how ordinary he looks, not the nightmare, monster I was expecting, just a very big, round faced, brown haired man. His face as expressionless and empty as his dark brown eyes. The grip on my limbs releases but is instantly replaced by the pressure of his forearms across my thighs and chest as he seems to be reaching for something across me. Straps to secure me, I realise and knowing I only have seconds to react, I brandish the wrench and as forcefully as I can, aim for his head.

Unlike my earlier kicks, the wrench connects with my target with a sickening crunch, and stops dead with a single blow.

The man rises, letting go of me, and looking at me with a mixture of anger, shock and confusion as blood pours down his face. He opens his mouth as though to speak but nothing comes out.

He reaches for my neck as his eyes glass over and he slumps forward landing half on me. His face is pressed directly onto mine for a moment before his descent continues as his legs give way pulling him to the ground.

I lie there for a second, before rising to sit with my legs hanging over the edge. I look down at him expecting him to get back up and attack me again, but then the amount of blood pooling around his head seems too much for him to get back up.

I've killed a man.

Shocked by how easily it happened, I shake my head in disbelief. It's never that easy to kill someone on TV or in the movies. And of course, the bad guy always gets up over and again, no matter what injury he has sustained!

I throw up over his prone hulk, a feeble, burning, acidic dredge of my empty stomach.

Unable to move or think, I stare at him a while longer.

Then I remember the other voice. It's only been a matter of minutes since the other person left. Either they heard my screams and will be here in seconds or they didn't but could still come back at any time. It's time to run again, if my body will allow it!

6.

Throwing caution to the wind I decide to make a dash for it. Racing up the stairs and out of the building, I head back in what I hope is the direction from which I came. My only thought being that if I can get back to the road I can hopefully follow it to civilisation and safety rather than risk another abandoned building. That is if I don't get caught by the other pursuer.

I feel no pain despite being fully aware of how battered and bruised my body is. My dislocated arm, flopping against my side as I can't even be bothered to hold it up, keeping my good hand free to provide support where else it is needed instead. Adrenaline has numbed me, giving me the strength to rush on. I'm sure the pain will hit hard when I am eventually safe.

Outside it is still just as cold and dark, much less time has passed that it might have appeared. I can't even imagine how long it must still be until the sun comes up. I've just got to keep moving, anything else is an unnecessary and potentially fatal distraction.

As I make my way back through the woods, I think I can hear things again, but I dare not waste any time thinking about it or looking back.

Eventually I exit back into what I hope is the same field from earlier, as I step out into the open I hear a loud bang, like a car exhaust backfiring and feel a sharp heat graze my good arm. Dropping to the ground I roll over in the grass attempting to get a look around me but seeing nothing but the shadows of the trees just behind me, and the outline of the bushes at the other end of the field. My arm stings and I can feel a wetness seeping through the sleeve of my ripped coat. Pretty sure I've just been grazed by a bullet, my resolve to get the hell out of here is heightened further. Getting back up to run doesn't seem like a good idea if I am being shot at, but I can't just lie here either.

Keeping low and in the shadowy edge of the trees for as long as possible, I crawl and drag myself along as fast as I can with an ever-weakening body, heading for the bushes and hopefully the road.

When I emerge on the other side of the bushes, I discover I have made it back to a road, but I can't see the cars or lay-by, so it must be further along, or maybe a different road?

As the bushes are taller than me, and running along a ditch, it makes good cover for me to stand again and run in the ditch alongside them. If anyone is in the field, they will not be able to see me unless there is a gap, and if anyone is coming along the road I might see them and be able to get help.

I am knocked to the ground as someone rugby tackles me from behind. I didn't even hear them coming. I begin my usual wriggling worm defence, as the wiry little man who managed to knock me down comes into view. He attempts to straddle me, a knife in one hand.

'Don't struggle love, need you in good condition,' he says with a raspy voice.

'Get the hell off me,' I yell in his face, bucking and squirming. I don't know where this confidence has come from, maybe killing a man will do that for you. He was a lot bigger than you, I think, about this scrawny runt on top of me. I throw my hips as high and hard as I can, and he is sent flying.

We both scramble to our feet, each as determined as the other. All my early fear gone in the face of confrontation. He lunges for me, and it's clear he is as poor a fighter as I am. He's all slappy, and slashy, with his knife held like he's going to butter a sandwich rather than stab me.

We dance around for a while in this pathetic manner, him swinging for me, me swinging back. A kick, a punch. Then he lunges for me with the knife held straight in from of him. I twist, and grab for his arm as he smashes into me. I've managed to grab his forearm and as we tumble to the ground I twist as hard as I can. We land with him on top of me again, and I steal myself to begin struggling again. Then I notice the look on his face, I've seen it before. Shock and disbelief. My hand feels wet on his arm and I remember the knife. One of us has been stabbed, and I don't think it's me. The man gasps, his mouth going like a fish as he seems to be unable to catch a breath. I realise the knife must have punctured his lung at the least. But as the wetness between us increases and blood trickles from his mouth I suspect an artery might also have been sliced as well.

It's slower this time, well at least it seems to be, I think as I watch the life drain from his face and feel his body slacken against me. I release my grip on his arm and shrug out from under him, wiping my bloody hand on his jacket as I use him to push myself up.

Funny, I don't feel sick this time, even though I have killed a second man. I just feel numb, like they weren't real, like none of this is real. In fact, it feels like I'm watching some low budget movie, where the heroine miraculously manages to defeat the evil guy out to kill her. Only there were two after me. That thought seems wrong. The gunshot, the sting in my arm. This guy had a knife not a gun, which means there must be one more out there. Fuck, I need to get moving again. I start to run along the ditch again, this time making sure I check back from time to time so I am not taken by surprise again. Although as the last guy has the gun, I don't think there is a lot I can do besides hit the ground if I see him.

7.

My advancement along the ditch continues unhindered, and I see that on the other side of the road there is an opening that could be a dirt or slip road. Crossing the road, the entrance transpires to be a driveway at the edge of a side road, where a sign declares the name Martac, a company I guess is further along the road. I can either enter the property here, were there are buildings close to the gate, or continue up the slip road and see what is up there. The former seems a better idea, who knows how far up the road I might need to go to reach anything else. Climbing over the gate it is apparent that the first buildings here are just old farm buildings and barns, used for storage so I pass them by.

Large machinery scatters the yard, including a yellow digger.

Passing round the end of the barns I am again faced with open land and bushes in the distance, no more buildings in view. I have lucked out again.

I hurry across the ground and push through the shrubbery.

A huge mound of what looks like gravel is directly in front of me, I can't make out how far it goes in any direction, so up and over seems the best route.

I clamber up the mountain of stones, slipping and sliding as there is nothing to get a grip on. With only one good arm and one good leg climbing it is not an easy task.

'Give it up, bitch?' I hear a thick black-country voice call from below me, a third man with a rifle slung over his shoulder is trying to follow me up the mound.

Encumbered by the rifle and the constant stream of moving shale from my own progress, he is getting nowhere. But, his pursuit means I must put more effort into my own climb. And as much as I can, I throw and kick stones behind me as I move to prevent him following.

I feel sweat around my hairline and running down my spine as I struggle to make my way up. My lungs protest at the effort, leaving me breathless when I eventually flop flat on my belly on the top. I look back first and see the man with the rifle is trying to aim at me from the bottom, he must have given up trying to climb up. Seeing that he can't get a shot at me from the angle we are both at he moves, I guess trying to find a way round the mound or better position to try and shoot me. Then he disappears, and a muffled echo of a scream reaches me, he must have fallen in a hole that was invisible in the darkness. I almost laugh to myself, I hope it was a deep hole, that he can't get out of and even better, that he is dead like his friends.

From up here all I can see are more and more mounds, blending into each other all around, but there does seem to be a track of tire marks running so far into the centre. This appears to be a quarry. I think to myself maybe the tracks will lead to the quarry offices, there must be some around here surely? And hopefully, now I am just trying to get help to get to a hospital and tell the police about the three men who were trying to kill me, whose bodies they can find where I've left them. That is, so long as the third man is dead, and doesn't get out of the hole he fell in.

Feeling a little safer than I have done all night, I allow myself a few minutes to just sit and get my breath back before doing anything else. When I get home, I'm going to quit smoking and get fit, I think to myself. I can't wait to see Kirsty, and everyone else I love. But first, I need a hospital, my wounds aren't life threatening but I do need some patching up, and plenty of rest.

I look around once more, and decide which direction to head down the mound to reach the track. Steeled with determination and hope I slowly, painfully raise myself up.

As I stand to run down the other side of the pile I slip on the loose stones.

I begin to roll down the mound.

As I fall a gentle rumble surrounds me as the mound begins to fall around me.

I instantly realise my mistake.

Panicking I attempt to stop my fall, but I am not rolling anymore.

Thrown forward, I am starting to sink, the stones, gathering speed, quickly cover my lower legs, falling around me like an avalanche.

In seconds I am buried up to my chest, the weight of the stones pinning me from moving far worse than the grip of the strong man.

Every effort to struggle and free myself just seems to be making me sink quicker, like being in quicksand.

I stop fighting as the rubble covers me only my head is now free, but the stones keep on coming.

An involuntary scream erupts from my mouth allowing stones to tumble in silencing me.

As I choke on the gravel filling my mouth, and my eyes become covered, darkness surrounds me.

My final comprehension is that this game of hide and seek has come to a tragic end, I don't know if I will ever be found.

ABOUT THE AUTHOR

This is the first published book by S.L. Grigg having previously written a popular blog on mental health, and having articles published by Mind, the mental health charity, and NHS England. Working for NHS England from a home in Bromsgrove, England, S.L Grigg lives with a partner and two adult children. S.L Grigg has studied everything from Science and Law, to Journalism and Pilates but writing has always been the greatest passion in S.L.Grigg's life.

24524490R00078

Printed in Poland
by Amazon Fulfillment
Poland Sp. z o.o., Wrocław